THE COINCIDENCE

ESSENTIAL TRANSLATIONS SERIES 21

 Canada Council   Conseil des Arts
for the Arts   du Canada

Guernica Editions Inc. acknowledges the support of
the Canada Council for the Arts and the Ontario Arts Council.
The Ontario Arts Council is an agency of the Government of Ontario.
We acknowledge the financial support of the Government of Canada through the
National Translation Program for Book Publishing for our translation activities.
We also acknowledge the financial support of the Government of Canada
through the Canada Book Fund (CBF) for our publishing activities.

FULVIO CACCIA

THE COINCIDENCE

*Translated from the French
by Robert Richard*

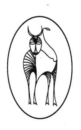

GUERNICA

TORONTO – BUFFALO – LANCASTER (U.K.)
2015

Original title: La coïncidence (2005): Les Éditions Triptyque
Copyright © 2005 by Fulvio Caccia and Les Éditions Triptyque
Translation copyright © 2015 Robert Richard and Guernica Editions Inc
All rights reserved. The use of any part of this publication,
reproduced, transmitted in any form or by any means, electronic,
mechanical, photocopying, recording or otherwise stored in a
retrieval system, without the prior consent of the publisher is an
infringement of the copyright law.

Michael Mirolla, editor
Guernica Editions Inc.
1569 Heritage Way, Oakville, (ON), Canada L6M 2Z7
2250 Military Road, Tonawanda, N.Y. 14150-6000 U.S.A.

Distributors:
University of Toronto Press Distribution,
5201 Dufferin Street, Toronto (ON), Canada M3H 5T8
Gazelle Book Services, White Cross Mills, High Town, Lancaster LA1 4XS U.K.

First edition.
Printed in Canada.

Legal Deposit – First Quarter
Library of Congress Catalog Card Number: 2014950180
Library and Archives Canada Cataloguing in Publication
Caccia, Fulvio, 1952-
[Coïncidence. English]
The coincidence / Fulvio Caccia ; translated from the French by Robert
Richard. -- First edition.

(Essential translations series ; 21)
Translation of: La coïncidence.
Issued in print and electronic formats.
ISBN 978-1-55071-873-7 (pbk.).--ISBN 978-1-55071-874-4 (epub).--
ISBN 978-1-55071-875-1 (mobi)

I. Richard, Robert, 1946-, translator II. Title. III. Title: Coïncidence.
English. IV. Series: Essential translations series ; 21

PS8555.A242C6413 2015   C843'.54   C2014-906224-9
                                                C2014-906225-7

JONATHAN HUNT

1

THERE IS SOMETHING NOT quite right about the man seated at the Café de la Poste. He looks like a heron that has somehow managed to fold its long slender legs under the table. And yet the simple fact that he is wearing moccasins makes him seem so familiar. One could easily imagine the acquaintances he might have, people who would know him, members of the new middle class that colonize the suburbs of our great cities.

He seems quite nervous. Obviously waiting for someone. His fingers are peeling the matches out of a matchbook. He takes from his pocket a tall notebook and begins to scribble something. He is hunched over the notebook like it was a microscope. Suddenly, he scratches out what he has just written. After which, he proceeds to fill two complete pages with his arabesque-like handwriting. He stops. Chews the end of his fountain pen. And then begins to draw a face. A man? A woman? Hard to say. He is plainly not very skilled at drawing.

He stares straight ahead, like a painter staring at a model seated just across from him. But there is no one there. Ever since he left Montreal, he has often been seen behaving in this strange manner.

Jonathan Hunt is a collector of dreams, something he owes to Clara – rather, he owes it more specifically to the bookshelf that now stands proudly in his room. A beautiful piece of furniture made of rustic pine and covering an entire wall. A small frieze decorates the contour. The whole has that look of solidity and clarity to it. Much like ... Clara herself.

"These shelves belong to you; it's up to you to fill them as you see fit," she had said to him one day pointing at the one empty shelf in the middle.

What she meant seemed obvious, well at least to him. It was then that he had decided almost idly to transcribe the dreams that came to him every night. He dreamed a lot, more than most people, he felt. To him, dreams were like some kind of intimate material that he could bend and twist into all sorts of shapes. At first, his goal had simply been to fill the empty shelves like a worker bee fills the honeycombs in a bee's nest. But slowly he had taken a liking to this little game of his. And since he was the rational type, he bought notebooks, tall notebooks, in which to record his dreams, notebooks that were all identical. Later, he even made a catalogue of sorts to bring some kind of order into this mountain of documents that he had accumulated.

He thought that one day the deep meaning of all this "junk", as he called it, would leap out at him. But for the moment, he was quite content to be doing Clara's bidding, be it in this somewhat complicated manner.

THE COINCIDENCE

Today though, he simply did not feel right about the details of the dream that he had just recorded. It was a recurring dream. But this time it contained a number of new details (the closing of a door, walking in the woods), details that seemed to call for an infinite number of new interpretations. Intuitively, he felt this dream contained a hidden clue as to the meaning of his life. But as often happened, Jonathan would wake up just as he was about to discover what that meaning was.

Jonathan laid traps for his dreams. He was like some kind of Amerindian putting snares all around his bed to catch them. In this way he had successfully "captured" more than six thousand five hundred dreams over the last fifteen years, stashing them in the dozen or so in-quarto volumes bound in real leather and which he stacked in an orderly almost fastidious fashion on that one bookshelf. The shortest of his dreams covered ten lines, while the longest took up over forty pages written in that very dense calligraphy of his. Jonathan would write these dreams under the "dictation of the unconscious," as would say. He even made a point of writing them down in this free, unbridled manner. He wanted to remain as close as possible to the "truth" of the dream. But in the end none of this had brought him one inch closer to anything resembling a revelation. The only thing he had to show for his persistence was this row of brown leather notebooks standing rather glumly on the shelf. Maybe this was all just another illusion that he entertained for lack of anything better. Jonathan had to face it: he was a man stuck in limbo.

And yet this state of limbo did not make him feel unhappy or unfulfilled. It had actually been useful to him during his rather brief career as a businessman. Sometimes, in those long business meetings, he would be filled with doubts to the point of becoming utterly speechless. And so a friend would give him ideas, word patterns, formulas to use in the complicated negotiations he had to undertake. But these helpful solutions never seemed to work. They could never turn him into a confident negotiator. That's not who he was. And so he remained plagued with feelings of uncertainty.

Of course the good thing now is he no longer needed to fight for his place in the business world. The savings he had managed to put way over time were quite sufficient to keep him going for the rest of his life. What's more, he was not a spendthrift and he lived alone. But at the same time he knew that even this stage in his life was about to come to an end. It had to. It's just that his life has become so routine-like. He needed a change. He wanted to shirk off that old skin of his before it stifled him. He did not want to remain trapped in the humdrum of things.

He knew he had a tool he could use anytime he wanted to put an end to it all. In his bookshelf, between two large volumes, there was a white metal box. This morning, Jonathan had opened it, taking out the gun that was inside it. With his right hand he spun the cylinder, and with an outstretched arm, he aimed the gun at some imaginary target somewhere before him. Then he turned the unloaded gun against his temple and went: "Bang! Bang!" He saw his reflexion like a phantom image in the window.

Jonathan suddenly felt a bit ashamed playing this childish game. No doubt that this was his way to keep his fascination for suicide at bay, a fascination that had gnawed at him ever since he had left Montreal. But enough if this. This coming

Whitsunday, he had decided, would be absolutely sumptuous – so there!

The phone rang. Jonathan went around the great rectangle of light that the sun had drawn on the wood-tiled floor. He skirted his way around the couch, went past the coffee table, and began rummaging beneath the cushions, where he finally found it. He picked it up but there was no one at the other end of the line. Had he been too slow in answering? Had he answered too abruptly, snarling as he was inclined to do? All he could hear was the crackling of a cell phone. He was about to hang up when a weak voice finally spoke his name.

The timbre of the voice surprised him: he suddenly felt as though he was back in Montreal. What's more, the caller had said his name in full, without the usual "Mister." The woman – it *was* a woman's voice – had obviously wanted to appear familiar to Jonathan, as though they had known each other from long ago. The voice was firm, not arrogant – this intrigued him. She was calling for the apartment. She asked if it was still available. Jonathan said yes. A meeting was agreed upon for later in the day. He did not want to give complicated directions over the phone, so he proposed to meet her at the subway station. Then he asked: "Do we know each other?" The woman answered, no, and hung up.

The call left him happy, almost excited, if a little perplexed. This feeling of euphoria had nothing to do with the fact that maybe someone was interested in renting his apartment. It came from the irrepressible, irrational feeling that *she* was coming back. Two or three things just seemed to come together: the way she rolled her "Rs," and that accent of hers both sensual and halting; and the veiled tone of voice that he felt he knew.

But there he was, daydreaming again. Time to snap out of it and get back to the real world. He slowly scanned the horizon through the picture window, taking in the cityscape. Over to the right, the green mass of foliage making up the Ramainville wood; out in front of him in the distance, the trembling form of Mount Valérien; a little off to the West, the Eiffel tower, its profile rising from the shadows; and finally the Montparnasse Tower flaunting its 54 floors of yellow translucent glass. This last part only made him want to vomit.

The one thing that really mattered to Jonathan was to remain bound to the present, with all its sounds and colours. It was as though he was always afraid of missing out on some magically sweet image that might suddenly materialize, right there before his eyes, out of the fragile morning light. Such was his daily quest: to grasp what was happening *now*. An absurd crusade when compared to the grand crusades led by mankind through the ages. This little crusade of his had but one goal: to feel detached from things in order to concentrate and hold on solely to the bare intensity of the sensations that those things aroused in him. Such was his aim. On this particular morning, another detail caused him concern: the acanthus leaves on the balcony were a little rusty. He really liked his "garden of Babylon."

It was his secret garden in the real sense of the word. He had chosen plants that generally grow along the shores of the Mediterranean. To this, he had added a hibiscus, an acanthus and a flamboyant, all of which ended up overrunning a good part of the terrace, invading it like so many "burning bushes."

He thought of the day when he had first visited this apartment. The light streaming in through the windows reminded him of the apartment he had almost bought in his native city. He had made up his mind very quickly. It took him little more than three hours, and he was already the proud owner of a large four-room apartment, with a breath-taking view of Paris and at no more than twenty-five minutes from the centre of the city by subway. Jonathan had a good eye for these things. He even felt that this had been the lucky shot of his life. He would often say so to his girlfriends, after they had made love. Sometimes when he felt depressed, he would remain for long hours on the terrace. He would smoke cigarette after cigarette while listening to his favourite piece of music: *Summertime*.

2

AT TIMES HE FELT he was turning into a bit of a crusty old bachelor. He was 39 years old, stood 5 foot 10, still thought of himself as "rather young." The proof: his flyaway locks and that intense, melancholy gaze of his, and of course he pleased women now more than ever. Let's say that he had simply *omitted* to get married. To anyone who was willing to listen he would say that he no longer believed in marriage. For him marriage was a kind of sacrifice where one of the partners gave up what he or she held precious solely for the good of the couple. And of course he had no desire to be the one to have to do this; he felt he had better things to do with his freedom than to lock it up in a relationship that would probably end anyway. Besides, he was too old, he was over the hill; this is what he would generally repeat to his girlfriends whenever they would try to get him to commit. He would add somewhat insidiously that "he was too respectful of women" to chain them down to this kind of domestic slavery. These discussions would always happen just when the relationship was about to go sour.

"When a woman gets too close to you, you become a living death." That's how his most recent lover, Gina, put it, before she left, slamming the door shut behind her. This had really gotten to him. More than he was willing to admit. But his freedom came at a price, one that he had to pay to that other self inside him, the one that continually asked, sphinx-like, the same question: "Who hunts the hunter?" Jonathan tried to make light of all of this. Preserving his freedom was the most important thing to him. He was aware of the paradox – his wish to live alone while courting women, but he could not bring himself to resolve it.

There was no doubt in his mind that his ex-girlfriend was right to some extent. In the end, his only true passion was his apartment. But it was a passion that was not without its problems. Especially now that he had to find someone who could look after it. This had become somewhat of a necessity after the death of his father some three weeks ago. There was all that complicated business surrounding the inheritance that just had to be settled. It could take weeks, even months. Jonathan had at first refused to take part in a process that, according to him, could only poison family relations. But his mother had reminded him that it was his duty. After all, he was the eldest of the family – even though he lived in another county, some 5,000 kilometres away.

To have to leave his apartment did not please him one bit. But the thought of leaving it empty at the mercy of thieves rid him of all of his shilly-shallying about renting it out to someone. And so he decided to try and make the best of a bad situation, especially since the candidates willing to live in his apartment were few and far between. The ideal candidate would of course have to be a "good person," someone with the "right profile." Jonathan simply could not stand the thought of entrusting his most precious possession to just anyone. That said, he would have been hard pressed to put a face on the ideal candidate. Obviously that person had to be financially solvent, but also share some of Jonathan's values, have the same habits; in short, be someone like himself: mission impossible if there ever was one.

3

CLUSTERS OF PEDESTRIANS MOVE, weaving a dark shimmering tapestry just outside the entranceway to the subway station. Cars honking, children squealing, playing. The crowds grow, clotting up, thinning out, as the trains come and go below ground. Like blood flowing in and out of a heart muscle, thought Jonathan. Centre town Orée du Bois is like a big bazaar, a chaos of sounds like some complicated drum beat, dingy hotels all round mixed in with new buildings with their swanky façades. Jonathan is busy striking all the matches he has on him. He suddenly realizes he has forgotten his billfold. A quick glance to his watch: he has been sitting in this coffee house for little more than ten minutes.

Another horde of transit users rushes up from the depths of the earth: a women stops at the exit, looks about. She is tall, blond. Jonathan stands up, but a stranger shows up and puts his arm around her. Jonathan sits down again, a bit put off. He takes a last swig of beer. Suddenly a frail voice, somewhat veiled, calls out to him: "You are Jonathan Hunt?" Two large eyes look straight at him. Jonathan says, yes. The strange woman's face lights up and she sticks out a small, well-proportioned hand: "I am happy to meet you. I am Leila Jones."

4

Jonathan's first reaction was to look her over, head to foot: she was wearing a flowered dress, with a man's jacket over it, a small overnight bag dangling on her shoulder.

"But you are not wearing leopard-skin pants," says Jonathan surprised.

The young woman bends her head as though checking, she slaps her forehead.

"Oh, I'm sorry. But I wasn't coming directly from my place. And I thought that it would not be necessary."

"How was I supposed to recognize you?"

"But people who are waiting for someone are always easy to spot, aren't they?"

Jonathan does not answer. Nothing irks him more than things that aren't according to plan. And to have a woman defying him made it all the worse! He bites his lower lip. The woman's voice that he had found so intriguing now sounds strange, even a bit absurd.

On the telephone, Jonathan had imagined someone he might have known, with long legs like Clara. And now he finds himself in front of a woman of average build with a mocking smile, a lingering sadness in her eyes, pretty enough, he supposes. Yet there was something fetching about her, something that might win him over despite his bout of ill humour: a certain way she had of bending her head. It made her look fragile and yet gave her an intensity of sorts. He asks her if she wants something to drink, but she shakes her head. It was as if someone had given the signal. Jonathan throws a bit of money on the table and gets up, ready to go.

5

As they walk from the rue du Pavillon de chasse toward Jonathan's apartment, they speak very little: just a bit of small talk to fill the silence, a chance for Jonathan to observe Leila closely. Her darting gaze gives her away. There is something at once animal and aerial about her. Over his lifetime, Jonathan had succumbed to the charms of many women, but none had what Leila seemed to possess. From that point on, Jonathan's attitude changes. He becomes friendlier and even starts behaving like some sort of a tourist guide: a role that allows him to be someone else for a change. And so there he is talking about the new rental apartments that "limit" the view one has of the Paris skyline off below, and he tells her about the project to repave the highway that goes all the way round city. He speaks of the l'Orée du Bois of yesteryear, when Paris seemed to calmly stretch off and away below.

The rue de Paris seems planted like an arrow in the body of the city, dividing it up into two parts. To the West, the houses of the working poor, built at the beginning of the last century near the sand quarry. And to the East, small houses recently built on a series of hills with brooks scattering off into the distance. These two "sides" come together on a higher ground, where Paris seems to reveal itself completely while at the same time keeping itself somewhat half-hidden behind some tall apartment buildings.

Jonathan is so much into his description of things that he does not even see the small red car coming up the rue des Compagnons, almost running him down. The car disappears in a squeal of tires. Jonathan lets out a vigorous swear word. But he regains his composure. He is calm again in large part thanks to the splendid panorama that lies before them. Below, the roves of Paris appear like sculpted waves, iridescent under the sunlight. To the right, one can make out the small forest that has given the commune its name. The young woman starts back a little. Jonathan smiles, then bursts out laughing.

Was it Jonathan's tall silhouette, his sardonic laugh, his impressive row of teeth that leads Leila to feel suddenly anxious? She is all at once a bit afraid of this man. His size, his dark gaze and his obvious need to please are simply not very reassuring, she thinks. She feels like a prostitute meeting a client or like a prey that has been tricked into retreating right into the predator's lair. She knows that her fear is completely ridiculous, but what can she do? She has to get a hold of herself if she is not to mess things up. She has to buy some time. A coffee house on a small square filled with sycamore trees finally allows Leila to escape to the washroom. When she returns, she looks up at the sky. There is a mass of white clouds, seemingly billowing higher and higher up against the sun.

"It's beautiful!" she exclaims. "How about a drink?"

Jonathan doesn't object, even if his apartment is just around the corner. He senses that she needs to feel right about this, needs to be reassured. And of course Jonathan loves to reassure women, especially this one who is a bit of a frightened doe.

6

Leila sits at a table under one of the sycamore trees; it's almost as if she is staking a claim. Off to the right, an iron gate leading to a manor house that has become a cultural centre of sorts. Through the railing, one can spot a birdbath hidden under a group of small birch trees. The shops are closing. The odd car looping about the traffic circle disturbs the quiet now and then. The small red car has somehow shown up again, its horn blaring. Jonathan frowns. He takes his smartphone from his pocket and snaps a picture. He sits down, checks the photo on the screen.

"You always do this?"

"Yes – to catch idiots who do stupid things."

"Are you a traffic cop?"

"If you like! I am a cop assigned to make sure silence reigns on our streets. Happy?" He stares at her almost defiant. "And what about you? What are you about?"

Leila does not answer right away. She bends her head.

"I am a nurse. A paediatric nurse."

"So you want to set yourself up here. That's good: there's plenty of work here."

"I don't want to work as a nurse; in fact, I don't want to work at all."

"I'm sorry, this is none of my business." Jonathan suddenly becomes more deliberate. "But I must warn you, the rental is just for a six-month period of time. And it's quite expensive here, not at all like Montreal. You know of course what the rental situation is like in Paris, right?"

"Yes, I know. Perfect for my needs."

"And ... what is it exactly that you hope to accomplish here?" It was as if he wanted to taunt her.

Now it was Leila's turn to laugh.

"Oh, don't worry: nothing illegal."

She stops, looks at Jonathan who seems expectant, waiting, and decides to tell him a little more.

"I want to become a theatre director, I'll be taking some classes."

"Okay ... that's strange."

"Just what are you trying to suggest?"

"Oh, nothing. I only meant that it's strange."

"... Strange that I abandon the stage of humanitarian catastrophe for a less dangerous stage, while thousands of refugees are dying of hunger – is that what you are thinking? Well, if you ask me, I think I deserve a break, nothing more. I don't have to justify myself, and certainly not to you."

"Listen, I *am* sorry, I didn't want to displease you. And anyway, it's really none of my business, right?" Jonathan is grasping at straws, searching for words. "...You ... you are putting thoughts in my head, intentions that simply are not mine."

She stares at him, puzzled.

"When I said 'it's strange,' I was not blaming you."

"…"

"Strange, because… well, there is this coincidence."

"What do you mean: coincidence?"

"That you are seated in that chair and that you want to be part of the theatre scene."

"I don't see what's so coincidental about that."

"You don't see it, do you? Well, of course you can't. It's just that you happen to be seated in the same place where Maria Casarès once sat – you know: the great French actress."

7

THERE WAS A REASON why Jonathan suddenly brought up the name of the great film actress. It was all part of a strategy. When Jonathan meets a woman he wants to seduce, he begins by surrounding her slowly, with his wit, with his old-world urbanity, in an effort to besiege her. It was how he worked things – it was his special "melody," as Horowitz, his ex-associate, had once said. But with Leila the situation is quite different. Each one of her moves, her every gesture seems planned. Even this little stopover at the coffee house seems to be part a program leading to some goal that Leila had already worked out in her mind. The only thing that Jonathan could be sure of is that Leila was slowly becoming enmeshed in his own destiny; it was as though she were his secret "music of the spheres."

Yet he would not have found this rather lovely musical phrase – Leila! – so attractive had there not been an aura of chance about it. For instance, this encounter was the fortuitous result of Jonathan's having to rent his apartment, was it not? After all, he could have chosen not to put it up for rent. And now the little ad he had placed in the paper had, again by chance, brought into his world this woman who is now seated before him, stirring her coffee. And so is the coincidence taking shape, *happening* right there before his eyes – just like in Jean Cocteau's film *Orpheus*. Already Jonathan was imagining Leila in the part played by Maria Casarès in that film from 1950, and what's more he could even see himself in the title role.

But he stops short of actually sharing these thoughts with her. Why? For a start, he thinks it rather silly for him to pretend to be an actor: he is no actor and he knows that. Instead, he prefers to see himself working away on the side-lines where he can more easily pull the strings, while Leila would remain thrust centre stage and into the limelight. And it is here that one of Jonathan's important character traits becomes palpable: superstition – Jonathan is, by nature, a superstitious man. For, in Jonathan's thinking, there is no such thing as idle chance. Chance always has a hidden design. In the end, things are somehow always *meant* to happen.

8

JONATHAN'S SUPERSTITION ALSO CAME with a passion for numbers. What fascinated him was how numbers resonate with this mysterious thing called destiny – *his* destiny.

"When were you born?" he asks somewhat offhandedly.

Leila looks at him, surprised.

"I was born on the 10th of January 1973 in Montreal."

"I thought you were born out of the county and only came to Montreal later."

"Well, if you want to know everything: it was my father who emigrated to Montreal," answers Leila a bit rattled. "And you?"

"July 4th 1964."

"In Montreal?"

"No, in a place called Hope in the States."

"Born on Independence Day under the Star Spangled Banner. Did you do this on purpose?"

"Pure coincidence!"

He laughs.

"My mother was visiting her family in Long Island. Her waters burst prematurely and she had to be hospitalized and that was it."

"Is this why your parents named you Jonathan, 'Blessed of the gods'?"

He looks at her somewhat perplexed.

"I know the dictionary of proper names," she says.

"But that's a completely different story. Names, I mean."

"It brought you luck?"

"Yes, at first" (he seems absorbed in his thoughts …). Everything good that happened in my life happened on a 4th: I launched my first business venture the day I turned twenty-two and I bought my apartment at l'Orée du bois on a 4th of June. My address is 4, rue du Pavillon de chasse. What's more: in a few weeks, I will be 40 years old!"

"It's a winning formula, then!"

"I know, these coincidences make you smile. As for me, I can never quite get over it, but I've finally come to accept it."

Was he talking too much? Maybe. But Jonathan was always like this: the eternally emotive guy always ready to let it all hang out.

At that very moment, Jonathan sees this image in his mind of the number four as a winged horse striving to rise above the chaos in its effort to hear the soft, mysterious music of the spheres.

"If we have a look at your date of birth, pick it apart, we always end up with the number four! Did you know that?"

Jonathan smiles a wide smile and says:

"Same thing with *your* date of birth."

Leila pulls a face.

"What am I to make of this?"

"That we're made for each other!"

"Well done," she chimes in, a bit saucily. "I didn't know you were such a whiz at numerology."

"I find it amusing, that's all."

Jonathan suddenly becomes serious. He presses the wind back button on his camera until the little red car shows up on the screen. The licence plate indicates that it's from Geneva. Jonathan finds himself adding up the numbers on the licence plate, and they too all add up to the number … four!

9

THE TIME HAS COME to leave. Jonathan insists on paying for the coffees. He summons the waiter. Leila can't help but think he's a strange fellow: charming, yes, but rather full of himself, narcissistic, and probably not easy to live with. And now there he is, walking a ways in front of her in one of the streets, a dead end. Leila takes in the quiet of the street, admires the luxury apartments lining it.

Jonathan's apartment is the one at the very top: "Penthouse with terrace," he brags, pointing it out. They go into the building and up the elevator. This "prow that sticks out over Paris," this "garden against the sky" pleases her immediately, almost despite the rather inflated descriptions that Jonathan had put into his ad. Happy with the effect, Jonathan shows her around. Bedrooms, workroom, washroom, living room, kitchen – just right, she finds, all the while trying to hide her delight.

"It's pretty big for someone living alone," she says as though speaking to herself.

"Room, lots of it, is the only luxury that I allow myself," Jonathan says, a bit vexed, and he adds that a lot people would love this apartment and feel quite comfortable living in it.

Leila feels she's made a blunder. She tries to retrieve the situation, and says that he is right and that she herself could not live in an apartment that was too small. And anyway, this place is exactly what she needs. She'll take it right away. What's more, she'll set up house alone.

Her voice lingers on this last word. And to boot, she offers to pay the whole six-month term in a lump sum. The roll of bills that she takes from her purse is additional proof that she means it. Jonathan's eyes grow big with astonishment.

"You are not afraid, walking around with all that money?" he asks.

"No, not at all," she replies almost defiantly.

Jonathan finds this mixture of daring and determination to be quite fetching. No doubt about it, this young woman is astonishing. He thought he was going to meet a young bohemian, without a red cent to her name. But instead here is a worldly-wise woman, who knows what she wants and who knows how to get it. She must be light as feather when she makes love, thinks Jonathan. But for the moment, it is best he stick to his role as owner. Would she happen to have any ID on her – to write up the contract? The young woman hesitates and then hands him her passport.

"You've been travelling for a while? ", Jonathan asks.

"Fifteen years!"

"And now, why the theatre?"

"It's what I've always wanted to do," she says somewhat anxiously.

"Sometimes events have us wander off the path we thought was ours ...," Jonathan adds, trying to put her at ease as she rummages for her passport.

One thing intrigues him: why is her given name Arabic while her family name is English?

Leila explains with a certain reticence that her last name is her husband's, an Australian doctor. There follows a confusion where Jonathan apologizes for being indiscreet when all he wanted was to know her maiden name which – he should have seen it – was written in big plain letters in her passport.

"Seyyad? Am I pronouncing it correctly?" Jonathan asks.

Leila says her last name carefully, and adds in a halting voice ... that it is a family name from the Middle East ... that her father was born there before emigrating to Montreal. Leila lowers her head and squeezes her left arm with her right hand as though to protect herself. She adds secretively:

"Names are never what they seem. It's the same with people."

And she raises her head, having gotten a hold on herself.

"What about yours? Is that your real name? I mean it's not an uncommon family name, though it's a bit rare in Montreal."

"Right on. My grandfather modified the family name when he emigrated. He wanted to begin a new life with a new identity."

Jonathan hands the young woman her passport. He is satisfied now that he has the upper hand.

"You know, we have something in common."

"And what would that be?" she asks.

"We both left Montreal at about the same time."

Leila does not answer, she simply smiles.

Could she take that apartment the day after tomorrow? The girl friend who lent her her studio is coming back early next week. Jonathan doesn't see why that wouldn't be possible. But suddenly he seems a bit bewildered: Where in heavens did he put that contract? He disappears into his office adjacent to the terrace. He can be heard foraging about. Time seems suspended. The curtains are wafting in the breeze. The acanthus leaves are rustling. Hibiscus flowers are leaning over and this woman, alone on the terrace, in the shimmering light, turning her head to look now at the Paris skyline, now at the sliding door. Their conversation picks up again through the drawn curtains.

"And ... you are going to put on a play, I suppose?"

"Yes, but it's not really a play, to tell the truth. It's something that has never been played."

"Who wrote it?"

"His name wouldn't mean anything to you."

Leila is walking back and forth, her hand sliding along the guardrail.

"What drew you to this particular play?"

"I don't know. Its strangeness."

But now that Jonathan asks, she feels like adding that it has to do with something like "infinite repetition." But she suddenly gets this sense of déjà vu. It is as though a thousand eyes were looking at her. It's a feeling that has come over her so many times before in her life. She feels a little dizzy. By chance, her hands grab on to the back of a chair, helping her to stay standing.

"Why strangeness?" Jonathan asks, completely unaware that Leila is shaken.

She finally pulls herself together and manages to explain that she had read this manuscript quite some time ago, she thought it had been lost, when, just recently, it came in the mail – in her name, but at that woman's place where she has taken a room.

"Nothing astonishing about that," Jonathan replies.

"Yes, but no one knows that I am here in Paris."

"Someone is looking after you?"

The young woman shrugs.

"Oh, let's just call it providence – or something like that."

"What's this manuscript about?"

"Travelling. Voluntary exile. A meeting. If this manuscript drew me, it is probably because it speaks of an experience that I myself have gone through ... Like you, I believe ..."

Leila is throwing Jonathan a line here, but for some reason he doesn't pick up. A drawer closes shut.

One can hear a distant strain of jazz coming from the cultural centre, on the other side of the street. Through the windows women can be seen exercising.

"You could take courses in jazz dancing – over there."

Those words are spoken up close. Leila turns. Jonathan is standing right beside her. He hands her the contract. He had probably been watching her for a while. His face is suddenly expressionless, cold. The only thing he has on his mind is that document. She signs at the bottom.

And so she will indeed be living in this apartment. How does one describe what binds an owner to his place of residence? The words "nostalgia," "emptiness," "floating" come to her mind. Those are the very feelings she had the moment she entered that apartment. Sure, she'll try to be careful not to let these feelings invade her life. Moreover, the fact that this apartment is so high up suits her perfectly. It gives her her solitude. Nothing else really matters. She squints because of the bright sun.

"Is this all that's needed?"

Jonathan smiles his predatory smile.

"Totally."

"We are now mutually bound," she says.

"You won't refuse a drink, will you?"

Jonathan raises his glass:

"May your play be a great success!"

And he goes bottoms up. Leila remains silent. She folds the contract carefully, puts it into her handbag and turns to have another look at Paris. The wind is blowing against the treetops, making them sway back and forth. Turning to face Jonathan, she asks:

"Are there any tennis courts close by?"

10

Jonathan suddenly pulls Leila against him. His tongue already on her cheeks, her neck, the nape of her neck. He breaks through the barrage of arms and hands. Touches her breasts. Holds her by the waist. Lifts her up. Takes her inside. Her forehead grazes the lintel of the sliding door, her arm brushes a floor lamp in the living room, then in the bedroom her shoulder hits squarely up against the edge of the pine bookshelf. Something pressing against her midriff, near her sex. His head. Searching. Her panties pulled aside. His tongue on her nether lips. Her soft wailing. Short cries of pleasure that are like pain. Now lying on the bed. Nervous fingers are taking off her clothes. He unsnaps her bra, takes off her panties.

Someone is on top of her, but it's not Jonathan. It's a lynx, a garden snake, something that's all over her body, which has become grassland, river, felled trees, oxbow lake – all round the mons veneris. The animal mouth brushes it. Then the sudden flood of memory, flowing back into her like the tide – waves, spaced out, then tightening, irradiating all around her sex. She didn't see her orgasm coming; she didn't see herself tip over out of present time. The air, the bodies mixed, woven, mingled. She is no longer here, in a specific place, but as though transported into some imaginary landscape. It seems to go on indefinitely. Another wave of sensation flows over her, over her clitoris, stimulating the nerves of her lower belly, tightening and relaxing alternately. He is inside her, pulling her into his movements. She submits, turning, twisting. Suddenly she becomes vague, absent. Like before. The man moving inside her is no longer Jonathan. Memories. She's on an island, it's wintertime …

Now it is she who wants to lead, to take control of their movements. To give them the breadth she feels she needs. She pushes her torso up tight against his. Their bodies fuse, heaving. To hold onto this pleasure, not allow it to escape. Not this time. Time becomes a slow circle, turning on its axis, present to past, in hard, compressed rhythms. Another orgasm rises, building up in concentric waves. She moans, her sighs as though sculpting the air.

Then again, the memories. A different winter landscape this time. It's early morning, the wind making the trees lurch. Where? Leila doesn't want to utter the name of the city. No, not that city. Suddenly, struggling with this broken piece of memory, wanting it to disappear, afraid it will bring back a slew of other recollections. Like bilge water. She's not ready for that, doesn't want it. Then, as though in some movie: snowflakes falling on a city. Christmas decorations, the flashing lights of dozens of police cars, ambulances. At that point, her orgasm floods darkly over her taut body, leaving her ashen, spent, broken.

11

JONATHAN AND LEILA ARE leaning against a tall fence, looking through it, their arms and hands held shoulder-high, pressing into the wire meshing. But to be able to make them out and to distinguish this particular fence from a prison fence or the fence surrounding a schoolyard, the camera would have to move back to give us some depth of field. This would allow us to see that the couple is actually looking at a tennis court. On the other side of the fence: four tennis players – two men, two women – hitting the greenish-coloured ball back and forth. They are all fairly good players, very spirited and putting on a pretty good show of it. The tennis players are drenched in sweat: they've been at it for a decent while now. A terrific backhand suddenly gets a resounding cheer from the three other players. But Leila looks away. She squints because of the sun just out from the clouds.

Jonathan lets go of the fence. They walk down along the courts. The storm is gathering in the distance. It probably won't hit this plateau with its sports complex. Jonathan wanted to show her the panoramic view of Paris that he likes so much. She doesn't say no. In fact, she says nothing. She allows herself to be led by this man's will, his desires. She feels he knows her. He had made love to her without speaking, without even kissing her. If he asked her to be her lover, she would not resist.

The couple is now walking along a soccer field. Joggers run by, t-shirts wet with perspiration. Jonathan and Leila step over the embankment. From there, they suddenly catch sight of the eastern side of Paris. The birds are singing loudly. The grounds where they are standing seem so cluttered – the wild grass washed by the sun.

Leila turns to look at Jonathan. Her eyes are bright. These grounds where they are standing are not especially beautiful, far from it. But strange as it may seem, rather than spoiling the surroundings, the greasy papers and beer cans lying all over actually make this place seem quite unique.

"From here the perspective is lower," explains Jonathan, forever the guide. "The tree tops are at the same level as your eyes – while, in Montreal, there is that mountain of course which dominates the whole city. And what's more, that mountain is at the centre of a huge plain."

Leila nods.

"At the time, I would walk on its crest. It seemed to go on for kilometres. I had my favourite promontory. The city below was smooth, black, horizontal. Against the light, I had the impression that Montreal was trying to flee, trying to escape some undefined threat of sorts."

"Because of the sky."

Jonathan does not need to be coaxed to explain what he means. For him, each place is like a painting that one has to describe and then interpret carefully, meticulously. He points out the block of turquoise sky against the browns and the greys of Paris. And then he draws her attention to that edge of the forest over there, green, fresh looking. The balance lies in this group of volumes, as in a painting by Nicolas de Staël. For Jonathan there is no mediation, no possible reconciliation between the city's horizon and the blue of the sky that swoops down on the city like a bird of prey. These two masses attract and repel each other as though locked in a singular yet silent combat.

She agrees. She recalls a high cliff road on that mountain in Montreal. From there one could plunge down into the city or fly up toward the heavens like Icarus. What had struck her was the light that was so white it seemed almost violent. It fascinates him that her description of the mountain that stands high over the city fits his own impressions exactly. It is as if Leila has managed to read into his past, as if she has taken the words right out of his mouth.

There is little doubt that he is falling in love with her. Before this moment, Jonathan was little more than a fog of possibilities, a web of intentions, more or less empty. He had even given up trying to understand his impulses, given up trying to make any sense of it. He was content with just being there, taking in the sensations, not bothering to give them a name, and in the end just shoving them in his leather-bound notebooks like the collector he was.

But in just these couple of days since he met Leila, he finds himself wanting for the first time in years to give some kind of shape to his life; to get the fragrance and the complexity of things back into it. All these impressions, that he'd been so busy stuffing into his tall notebooks, might finally give up their meaning.

The notebooks could then serve as a crossover, a bridge toward something else, something fuller in terms of his own life-potential. This is what Leila's presence seemed to be allowing. Slowly but surely his *story* seemed to be picking up again, getting under way once more after such a long interruption. Jonathan would now have a goal. He knows that the outcome is inescapable, just like the events which, back on that fateful December day, had him ready to leave at a moment's notice. And in this process, Leila is like an acid bath that brings out the darker colours on the photographic paper. And so one "sweet image" had led to another. It had been a while since he had thought of memory as something that could free him from his anxieties. And now the "dear sweet image" he had hoped for was taking shape right before his eyes. It was even speaking to him.

Jonathan turns to look at the horizon; he is listening to the distant clamour. The sight of Paris is really secondary. It's of no real concern here. What matters is this feeling of abandon, of freedom that seemed to dominate on this rather plain and cluttered gypsum hill.

It would seem that man and nature had agreed to leave it deserted and bland. And it is precisely this neglected look that gives this site its alluring strangeness. The young woman is saying this to Jonathan who lowers his eyes. Everything melts away. All that remains is the singing of the birds, the whistling of the trains far off in the distance. Below, the garbage trucks are growling, compressing the trash – and there is that little red Orion car again, the same one as on the square, heading off at top speed, backfiring as it disappears ... Then: nothing. Silence. But the quiet is deceptive. The calm before the storm. How long will this silence last? A few minutes? Hard to know. It's at this point that Jonathan hears his "music," as he secretly calls it. It starts with a distant vibration, very faint. Then it becomes a bit clearer.

"Can you hear it?" he asks.

Neither of them moves, their senses watchful, listening.

She smiles: "I think I can. It's like a cow-bell, like the kind one hears in high mountain pastures."

Jonathan smiles too: "Yes, it's my little 'music of the spheres'." He shakes his head and adds: "But I can't seem to be able to find where it's coming from."

12

"Come!"

And there goes Leila in the opposite direction from where they came. Jonathan is surprised. What's gotten into her, almost insisting that he follow her like that? He understands of course that she wants to find where that mysterious sound is coming from, its source. She goes straight ahead, as though guided by a magnet. She is moving so fast that Jonathan has trouble keeping up.

They run across a grass clearing, and go up a steep slope to a promontory. They run over the long grass. From the summit of the valley, at the foot of which runs a bunch of underground high-tension cables, the couple enjoys a lovely view of the Eastern part of Paris. But Jonathan has no time to look at it. The couple goes down the slope under the branches and finds itself in front of another park in the middle of which runs a road. The sky is still vibrating to the clanking of the mountain bells.

"It's coming from over there."

She points at the woods before them. Her companion eyes the dark green mass behind the fence. He is wary, cautious. Access is forbidden. He shows her the sign that warns against the possibility of sinkholes. These woods are filled with them. Jonathan remains planted in front of the fence, not daring to go any further. Beyond, a tangle of tree trunks, covered in ivy and moss, form a wall of vegetation. The wind is stirring the whole of this impenetrable mass. The sound of the bell has ceased. All that remains is the distant bustle of the city. Leila walks along the fence carefully examining its base. Suddenly she stops and disappears in the vegetation. She reappears motioning to Jonathan to come over.

"This way. There's a hole!"

"But … But it's dangerous!" warns Jonathan. Leila shrugs her shoulders and dives into the opening. Though a little scared, Jonathan decides to follow her.

"You are just a scaredy-cat, " she says brightly.

"Stop teasing me. This place is like Swiss cheese. An old legend has it that a couple, lovers, got lost here, and no one ever saw them again."

"Huh, maybe that's us?"

Jonathan stops frowning. They have switched roles: he should have been the guide, but now it is she who is forging ahead. It would seem that the daring of his new tenant knows no limits. In front of them, a bramble bush is blocking the view. The trees look like scarecrows. Which is what they are: their purpose is to keep people away more efficiently than all of those official warning signs. This part of the woods has not been cleared in ages; Probably not since the quarry they've stumbled on was abandoned.

With the help of a stick, Jonathan tests the ground in front of him like a blind man. The usual landmarks he relies on have vanished: he can just make out the apartment towers behind him. But now that he has wandered into this thicket he feels the woods are swallowing him up whole, as if his "little music of the spheres" has trapped him in its hoops. He feels like he is exploring the hidden face of the moon – better still: limbo. As for Leila she is hopping out in front like a kid goat.

"Where are you taking me?" he cries out.

She does not answer. There are no sounds save for the wind brushing against the grass. Leila's brazen behaviour strikes a familiar chord in him, one that he thought he had forgotten. Details from his dream come back to him. It was as if a new island was starting to emerge, smoking from an oily sea. In this strange place, he rediscovers some old impressions that make him doubt his own existence. Jonathan tries to get a hold of himself. He does not want to start building castles on the shifting sands of appearances. How many times before has he ended up trapped like this? How many different personas of himself has he sent off into this world, each one on some improbable mission? Hundreds – if not more. He sometimes actually believed in some of these personas, going so far as to identify himself with them. But then everything would crumble to dust.

Once, only God or poets managed to grasp this huge mass of destinies like a ball of wool, picking out of it almost by chance a few strands that might serve as examples. Today, when everyone is being watched, where the webcam replaces the eyes of God, and where each individual aspires to his 15 minutes of fame, this need to be seen has become very banal. Jonathan's anxiety could of course come from the fact that he no longer knows if he is just dreaming or if he is the mere product of someone else's imagination, someone he would have to acknowledge in order to find his way out of this labyrinth of vegetation. For the moment, he moves forward in this downy, vertical uncertain mass. The storm is fast approaching, but suddenly he's lost sight of Leila – where is she? She had up to then been just up a bit of the way ahead of him! He would have liked to kiss her again, make love to her slowly.

He calls for her once, twice, three times. No reply. Where the devil could she be? Suddenly, he hears a muffled, dull thud, followed by a lengthy moan. He comes closer, pushes away the long grass with his stick, like they do in those adventure films he likes so much. A muffled voice, painful, distant, comes from somewhere underground. His fears are confirmed. Jonathan bends down over a hole in the ground, hidden by the tall grass. In the dark, at about a dozen metres below him, a shadow is moving.

How in heavens will he get her out of there? Jonathan looks around and sees a long branch that might be of use. He reaches to grab it. It could be that his movement was too quick, too brusque or maybe it was the ground that simply gave way under his weight. Whatever is was Jonathan falls into the crevasse. He lies there unconscious.

How long was he out? One second, five minutes, he doesn't know. What he does know is that Leila's beautiful face is looking down at him.

Jonathan gets up slowly. Luckily a carpet of leaves had cushioned his fall.

"I had warned you," Jonathan says sharply.

Leila bites her lip. All around them, the darkness seems so humid. The light filtering into the crevasse illuminates a tall cone of earth, some fifteen metres high, surrounding a tree. It must have been the branches of that tree that had covered the hole, hiding it. It is there that he and Leila fell. There are so many cave-ins like this around here. To climb the cone of earth and clay was just impossible, there has to be another way out.

"What are we going to do?" Leila asks.

"I don't know," he says, flicking his lighter open to be able to see in this darkness – then under his breath:

"… And to think that I left my cell phone at home."

He turns to Leila:

"You wouldn't happen to have one by chance."

Leila shakes her head.

"Just as I thought," he says, scanning the blackness around them.

"We can try to call for help, perhaps some passer-by will hear us," Leila says.

"No, that's useless. This place is completely isolated. No one will hear us."

Leila wants to be forgiven. She lights her own lighter, moves forward, resolute, slowly brandishing left to right this measly torch of hers. She does not smoke and so congratulates herself for having kept this lighter, which she found on the street. But the flame begins to flicker, weakening.

"Look, there are some passageways."

In the shadows they can see the mouth of a tunnel.

"That's not unusual: we are in an old quarry," Jonathan replies, irritated.

"Maybe one of them could lead us above ground somewhere."

"I suppose nothing to lose now that we are stuck here. We've only ourselves to blame. I might as well go first."

His voice has softened. He pauses, then adds:

"Whisper in my ear if you want to talk to me from now on."

They both go into the tunnel. Jonathan has Leila stay right by his side so that their combined lighters can give out a bit more light. They keep moving forward, slowly. Jonathan feels her breath on his neck, her skin quivering against his when they brush against each other.

They walk in silence over a long distance. The only sounds are those of their steps as they move ankle-deep through the shallow pools of water. Drops falling from the roof of the cave, making steady pocking noises all around them.

"We seem to be approaching another crevasse," Leila says.

"We'll see. Are you cold?"

But Jonathan realizes that the question is utterly silly. Poor Leila is shivering. He covers her shoulders with his jacket. To lighten things up, Jonathan tries to explain the origin of these vibrations, the origin of this little music. Could it be caused by a natural phenomenon? Or maybe it's the wind blowing in the ruins of some abandoned broken down industrial building. It is then that the huge manor house at the far end of the park comes to his mind. It once belonged to some aristocrats. Today it is all boarded up. Maybe a bell had been forgotten inside and the wind is causing it to vibrate at times.

"Maybe this vibration you hear is actually a combination of sounds, a mixture, like the colour black which is the concentration of all colours," Leila says.

"Like in Hell?" Jonathan answers.

"It is by going through Hell that Dante finally ends up in seventh Heaven," Leila replies.

"Going to those lengths just to see again a woman who had died," Jonathan says as though speaking to himself.

"And to see her face again: that's no a small accomplishment."

"But Dante is a little short for words when he finally sees God's face, right?"

"One must be struck dumb, unable to speak, when one comes face to face with God. And anyway, it's Beatrice who helps him find his way to God."

"Hell was not so nice to Orpheus!"

"Because he turned to look back when Eurydice called out to him. He wasn't supposed to, he should have just kept looking straight ahead."

"Just as I thought, even in Hell, there has to be an old wives' tale – always a woman or someone's wife in there somewhere."

Leila shoots him an angry look. Jonathan is visibly happy to have gotten her riled up.

"How do you know that the sound of the bell comes from this wood?"

Leila lowers her eyes and raises them again.

"It's because of the dream!"

Jonathan begins to walk slower, as the words start to flow from Leila's lips.

"In this dream, I am walking in a dense undergrowth like this one, yes, just like this one, when suddenly I spot an empty wallet, its contents spread all over. There is also an envelope containing a manuscript. The ID card belongs to a man from another country; although his name is familiar, but I am unable to recall it. On the other hand, I look at the photo on his identity card. There is gleam in his eye that I find striking; a profound gaze, infinitely black like an abyss. I look around: I find that I am near a forest. Suddenly a man comes walking in my direction. He is dressed in black. He seems to be returning from a restaurant in town. He is looking for something, carefully inspecting the ground. The ID was his. I said his name in the dream and surrendered his documents to him. His face lights up and he says to me: 'You have finally recognized me.' He takes my hand and brings me to an opening in the fence. When I woke up, I had forgotten both the face and the name of the man. The only thing I remembered were the first words of the manuscript that he had left with me: 'Night abyss.' The following day, after the dream, I found the manuscript addressed to me in my girl friend's mailbox where I was staying."

Leila is watching Jonathan, wondering what his reaction will be. Jonathan's gaze deepens as though lost in thought.

"I should maybe state right away that the dark handsome individual was *not* you."

But Jonathan isn't saying anything. He is ruminating, idly massaging his chin with his left hand. "This dream has all the characteristics of an unresolved enigma," he murmurs, satisfied. He looks at her, a knowing smile on his lips.

"I think that in your heart of hearts, you know the real identity of this man. At an opportune time, I am sure that his name will reveal itself to you. I really think that, and you will then be able to fit your dream in the seventh category."

"And after that?"

"Well, this means that your dream will have revealed itself to you and that you will finally be able to interpret it."

"How do you even know that?" she asks.

Suddenly, they hear a loud booming sound. Jonathan asks her to remain silent. They walk faster. At the end of the tunnel, they can see a feeble light. The passage has widened. It even seems that someone lives there from the looks of it: the mattress on the dirt floor, the empty bottles of wine, and the stench. It's probably a makeshift shelter for some homeless man. They finally emerge near a promontory. The entrance is half-blocked by a large piece of cardboard.

"Will you look at that," Jonathan says. "We've somehow come full circle."

In front of them, lower down, there is a clearing where a circus tent has been raised. Ponies are grazing in the tall grass. Further off a llama is doing the same thing. The couple clambers down the slope. Leila doesn't bat an eye. When an elephant lumbers over in their direction, she goes up to it, pats its trunk. The animal then turns and walks away as though this was all quite normal.

"I've lived in Uganda," she explains when she sees Jonathan's surprised look.

"Why did you come back?"

Leila pauses before answering.

"Because war broke out again."

They go by the circus tent. The wind sweeps up the leaves lifting them high above their heads. The shadows are playing with the light. The sky resembles the ceiling of a cathedral with its columns of light. In this undergrowth, Leila and Jonathan are like the improbable figures in an open-sky nave that is constantly changing. The silver-grey layering of the sky strikes a contrast with the black electrically charged horizon. The wind picks up, the leaves rustling in the trees. Up above, the soccer field has emptied of its players.

"This time we won't escape the rain," Jonathan says.

Leila scans the horizon.

An emotion suddenly seems to make her glow. Jonathan tries to identify the strange yet subtle fervour that is suddenly emanating from her. "Nobility of the soul": that's what it is. It's like an inner strength that he feels in her and that both attracts and rejects him. He feels he needs to do something: take out a handkerchief, take her in his arms. Without his really being aware of it he begins to kiss her, at first softly, then with passion. Her lips have a slight taste of vanilla. Her tongue responds to Jonathan's hardy attacks, drawing her into a sort of delicious, sweet abyss. Her mouth is a fairy-like cavern.

Jonathan is overcome by a warm feeling. Even the storm seems like a harmless lovable symphony off in the distance. Leila's body is like a musical instrument in this moment of grace. But then she pushes Jonathan back. She is ambivalent, wanting him and yet wishing he was no longer there. Nothing seems to matter save the desire slowly rising in Leila's lithe waist, rising in Jonathan's long, dry silhouette. They are like two racing cars on a head-on collision course. Two bodies, two cannibalistic mouths, trying to devour each other. With his hands, Jonathan feels the body of this reed-like woman. She bends, then suddenly stops:

"Not here."

She speaks these words with a kind of authority, though not harshly. He helps her get up. The first raindrops form little craters in the dust covering the road.

13

IN THE DARK, THE neon light is sizzling, shedding from the ceiling a cold light onto their rain-soaked hair. Their two bodies seem stuck together. Jonathan's hands are on the young woman's waist. He kisses her in the neck, in the ear, as the elevator of the 4 de la rue du Pavillon de chasse takes them up in a horrid metallic jangle of noise.

Jonathan opens the door to his apartment. His hand is searching around for the light switch. He flicks it on. But the light doesn't last. A huge deafening roar makes the apartment shake: lightning has struck close by. Leila escapes, like a gazelle in the dark, and plants herself in front of the sliding door, its watery surface reflecting the myriad tone colours of the city. The downpour sweeps the street. The rooftops shine like the scales of a serpent. There is another crash of thunder, like a volley of shots in honour of some pagan god. In the distance, a slender band of sulphur yellow creates a curious ambiance, suspended between heaven and earth. The low clouds seem massive. The power is still out. Matches crack and soon little haloes of light dance in the four corners of the living room. Desire has not melted away – it's still there, lying in wait.

Jonathan drapes a bathrobe over Leila's shoulders. But she seems oblivious of this thoughtful gesture.

"I am hungry!" she exclaims.

Jonathan laughs, then goes to the kitchen wiping his eyes with a towel. One can hear the sound of pots and pans being taken out of the kitchen cupboards. Water running from a tap. Jonathan's voice is gobbled up in the noise of the hair-dryer. The conversation over dinner is banal. This reassures Leila. It is as if they had been living together for a while now ... They are acting like a real couple. Her imagination goes wild: they have children and these children are now off to visit their grandparents. This evening, they wanted to go out, but the rain surprised them ...

Stop! Leila wonders why her mind gets all wound up like this. She has no logical explanation to offer. But now she has the feeling that she has jumped into another time period. Everything seems to have a rhythm and a contour that bespeaks of some other present.

Leila has finished drying herself off. She comes out of the washroom, her heart lighter. Her hand glides along the back of the leather settee. The storm is receding. The city in the distance is a chaos of shimmering lights. She knows now why this place appears so familiar to her. It's the way the apartment seems to be looking down on the horizon. It all comes into sharper focus now: the house in the trees. With her brother. She closes her eyes as though trying to hold on to the emotions that this brings back. Jonathan has some of the same traits as her brother: the way he looks at objects or at people, and there's this particular habit he has of bending his head to one side … Can she trust these feelings that are triggered by him?

With time, she has learned to be wary of her first impressions. But today there is something inside her that does not want to be mistrustful. Something deep inside her. She feels that her own abyss reflects that of her new companion. This feeling of being so at ease in his presence is for her proof of that. But how can one really know that? Enough! The only important thing is the present, this moment – or rather this absence of time that she is receiving like a gift, like a tribute to what she is. Nothing else counts.

"What are you trying to prove with your theatre play?"

Jonathan's question draws her out of her dreamy state. The kitchen door has remained open. She hesitates.

"It's not a play."

"But you *are* staging it."

"Yes."

"So it is a bit like yours."

She reflects.

"The text talks about something that comes from the outside."

"What do you mean?"

"A stranger, someone unknown, and this is what gives the text its unity."

"Go on."

"He is the one who steals the show. He turns the whole family upside down. And each individual in that family finds him or herself confronted by their own listless existence.

"It's a cataclysm?"

"It's about being exiled, but no longer seen as a fatality: more of an intimate or inner experience."

"But the fact is that the experience of exile has always been around. Nothing new there. That's what the myth of Cain and Abel shows quite clearly."

The speed of their spontaneous back and forth banter surprises them both. As though Jonathan had been thinking of nothing else all these years; and in a certain way, that was the case. And so their incipient relationship moves to a new unknown level that each must now somehow defend.

"One must not confuse the nomad way of life with having to go into exile," she says.

"Oh, really!"

"The person who chooses to go into exile is someone who is sedentary, but who has been forced by circumstances to hit the road. Cain was a peasant who becomes a nomad after killing his brother. To expiate his sin, he will be condemned to found cities in which he will not be allowed to live."

"I knew it! When you really look at it, he's the more interesting character of the two brothers. Not this lazy good for nothing, Abel, who has done little else than eat the dust of the roads all his life, and who was quite content to immolate a few sheep now and again to obtain God's favours.

"That's true. You're right."

"And conquests and empires and all of that, they're not everything," Jonathan says, annoyed.

"Famines, epidemics, natural disasters, they also make people leave and go into exile – Don't you think I know that?

Catastrophes just happen and people react. Ideology has nothing to do with it in such cases."

Jonathan emerges from the kitchen with his apron, a kitchen knife in one hand and a tomato in the other.

"That's all very nice, but how is this supposed to apply to someone like me?"

As he speaks, he puts the blade of the knife flat on his heart. To see him come out of the kitchen like this makes Leila jump. But she manages to steady herself.

"Very simply because exile, immigration are now becoming the rule."

Leila stops, marshals her arguments. She feels she has to be as convincing as possible.

"Let's take you as an example: you live in a country which is not your country of birth. Was your father born in the same country as you? Maybe, maybe not. With your grandfather the chances are even slimmer. It was the same for me. My father moved to a different country. Now it's my turn to live elsewhere."

"In my case," Jonathan says, "there is no comparison: I chose to leave. Nobody forced me."

"This self-imposed exile of yours doesn't change a thing, even if your aim is to blend into your new country. And anyway, I don't think you've been able to accomplish that, at least not completely." She pauses as though she were trying to come up with something.

"You have to understand what I am getting at here. It is perfectly normal to want to leave and, even if this is just a personal decision, it says something about the discontent or the discomfort one feels: I am talking about the rift there is between a particular individual and his milieu. I'll give you an examples taken from the manuscript."

She rummages around in her bag and takes out a crumpled envelope, out of which she extracts, triumphant, a pile of tattered, dog-eared papers. But she can't seem to find the passage she is looking for. The bulk of the manuscript is made up of a bunch of pages, most of which are blank or on which the writing has been crossed out, deleted.

"Strange … I thought … I must have grabbed the wrong document on my way out and left the other one behind."

She is dismayed. She puts the document back in the envelope and, fed up, throws the whole of it onto the small table in the living room. She fears she's been pretentious. Jonathan is perplexed, he bends his head, lifts it up again.

"And what about you, why did you leave?"

She sighs heavily.

"I don't want to talk about it – not now."

She walks up to the panoramic window. Outside, the light is tinted ochre, with green reflections of ivy on the wall. At the horizon, the rumbling of the thunder has disappeared in the distance. The clouds are criss-crossed by lighting here and there. She suddenly feels awkward: Has she been talking too much or maybe not enough? The African music coming from the community centre just out in front is again audible. She slides open the door leading to the terrace. Syncopated rhythms and percussions mix with the faint light of the candles projected onto the walls. Leila wants to forget everything. Start all over. What got into her to talk so much, like a chatterbox?

Jonathan remains standing in front of her, his arms hanging, intrigued.

"It's ambitious," he says. "But in the meantime, how are you going to make a living?"

The question bothers her, it irritates her. She then begins relating, word for word, the interrogation that her father had forced her to undergo when she had told him of her decision to continue her studies. In this manner, her father was telling her that she could not count on his support. It was not so much the financial aspect. Nor was it because she is a girl, a woman: he had had the same attitude in the case of her older brother. This attitude was the repetition of a more ancient refusal: the refusal that her grandfather had served her father in a similar situation. The road leading to knowledge had been blocked for him, too. But her father had held on, going so far as to choose exile, to go far away, and in this manner to break with destiny and with the ignorance of the fathers. But at what cost? It was this part of her memory that Jonathan's harmless question had brought to life again.

She could have sidestepped the question. But instead of that she gets caught up giving complicated explanations. Her voice is higher pitched than usual, feigning a theatrical indifference, as she mentions the small jobs, the classes she gave, the translations she had done, the proof reading and even telling him about the small amount of money which she had managed to save up over the years. She gives tons of details just to justify herself, as though it were her own father who was there demanding explanations. She lowers her head, mumbles some vague excuses. Jonathan has the decency not to comment. A long, low whistle rises from the kitchen.

14

THE WATER IS BOILING furiously in the saucepan, the lid dancing over a cloud of steam shooting off in all directions. In the glow of the candles, Jonathan finishes cutting up the tomatoes into tiny cubes. He adds garlic, spices and small slices of basil leaves. When the moment is right, he adds the hot spaghetti to the diced tomatoes with its perfume of olive oil, a recipe that he inherited from his grandmother. Leila insists on setting the table in front of the picture window. She wants to look after the coffee. She runs some beans through the old hand-run coffee grinder suspended above the oven. The delightful aroma incites her to ask him where he got it. But the word used to designate a coffee merchant escapes her. She makes a few unsuccessful attempts to say the word. Finally, Jonathan whispers the word to her. "Tom," she says to herself. The third time, her lips form the syllable silently. Busy mincing the herbs, her host doesn't see her face reddening ...

Nor does he see the blade of the knife coming too close to his hand. In this half-light, something like this is bound to happen.

A sudden cry in the silence, followed by a swear word. Jonathan comes out of the kitchen, sucking at his wounded index finger. She insists on examining the wound, and heads straight for the washroom. In the glow of the candle, the pharmacy reveals more than just the first aid kit she is looking for: a whole array of anti-depressive drugs.

She doesn't breathe a word, content to bring what is needed to bandage up the wound. This reminds her of old and familiar gestures that she accomplished day in day out. How many skeletal bodies and bloodied limbs had she nursed? Looking back, her life seemed like such a labyrinth. All those years gone up in smoke. A decade of missions and assignments and of pain flashes by in her tired memory. And now she is face to face with her mirror: Jonathan.

15

THE GLOW OF THE candles cuts out two hieratic silhouettes against an all-lit-up Paris skyline. It makes for a strange contrast: black on a background of stardust. A constructivist painter would have chosen to represent the scene under the guise of a black square at the centre of which radiates a luminous halo, itself contained in a vast rectangle constellated with luminous dots. But painting is the last thing on the couple's minds. They eat, swallowing slowly. The scene might even seem funny with Jonathan and his wounded finger wrapped and sticking straight up. But a curious air of uneasiness has descended upon them.

To break the silence, Jonathan decides to pursue the discussion about exile, bringing to it this time his theme of predilection: dreams. He goes on a bit with a bunch of pseudo naïve questions. What do people leaving their country in order to settle elsewhere dream about? Leila is not fooled by this little game of his. She quite simply ignores his questions. She takes care to explain that, for the author whose play she is staging, the dreams of returning to one's homeland are as numerous and diverse as there are immigrants on earth. She gives one of her own dreams as an example, a dream in which a man is compared to a battery that is charged up with the particular *earth forces* that emanate from whatever place he happens to be. When those forces are as it were too "positive," the individual's magnetism dissolves back into the earth beneath; if, on the other hand, they are too "negative," this magnetism evaporates up into the atmosphere. This quick exchange of views has helped clear the air. Suddenly she asks with that sense of wry irony that is so characteristic of her: "And by the way, you did not tell me about your dream."

Leila's words come to Jonathan as though filtered through the light of the past. In the half-light, the room seems to beat to the rhythm of Jonathan's heart. It is as if the space becomes suddenly filled with ionized currents. He is there, and yet not really there, not really present. His tongue articulates a few sounds that have become strange even to himself. Jonathan sees himself once again, in his mind's eye, his elbows propped up on the railing of a small balcony. He is looking down at a deserted schoolyard below. He is no longer in Paris, but in Montreal, in his old apartment. The apartment is empty, bathing in a soft translucent light, cardboard boxes piled in the corridor. The pulsating beat is growing louder. He is about to leave: the house is being condemned. But a feeling of happiness has taken hold of him. A red car stops in the street below. It's the taxi he'd called for. Jonathan puts into the trunk of the cab the cardboard boxes containing all of his belongings. He takes a seat in the back and night falls almost instantly. Like in the tropics. Inside, there is a woman, whose milky body, almost naked and covered in a rash, makes him want to throw up. He is left speechless.

"You are going to make me lose all my clients," the driver says reproachfully to the woman. Jonathan has heard that voice before. No wonder: it's the voice of that man he'd run across briefly, earlier in the day. This was ten years ago.

"What are you doing here?" asks Jonathan surprised.

"Why, I'm working," the man answers.

The taxi takes off, but the driver suddenly puts on the brakes: a new client. A young man wearing a pair of faded jeans steps in. Beard, long hair, a big backpack slung over his shoulder. Jonathan is forced to sit even closer to that woman. She must have some kind of skin disease, which makes it hard for her to wear clothing. Jonathan can't make out the woman's face. The car accelerates, wanders through the Eastern part of the city, which is like a huge techno-punk bazaar filled with garish neon billboards, before finally escaping by the grand boulevards that lead outward and around the city.

The taxi is now moving on a three-lane interchange. Beneath the thoroughfare, the city appears like a horizon of colourless concrete cubes. It is hot. The car descends from the elevated highway and enters into the suburbs where the landscape changes completely. Here in these streets, you won't find any of those sleek powerful sedans – just a shamble of old carts and rickshaws and broken down trucks ... Jonathan's attention is drawn by the curious activity of workmen moving blocks of wood as though they were made of straw, piling them up into unstable and coloured pyramids. Heaven knows why, but the idea flashes through his head that he has somehow landed in the suburbs of the city of Lagos.

Then it's the traffic jam and the insufferable heat and the dust and all that mad honking. The engine is heating up badly, until finally the car has to be abandoned by the side of the road. The occupants get out and walk under the hot sun and finally go their separate ways. The young hiker decides to try and thumb a ride; the taxi driver does the same. The two who remain behind wave at them. The mysterious woman takes a blue opaque veil out of her bag, and covers her face with it. Slowly, the suburbs transform themselves as if by magic into an exotic savannah with its long tall grasses and isolated trees; a river winds it way through it. A young African woman in a loincloth has created a narrow beach made of fine white sand.

To cool himself off, Jonathan plunges into the river, its waters finely honeycombed by the tides. The water is silky and transparent. He swims with delight and notices that the mysterious woman has plunged into the river near him. The blemishes that pockmarked her skin have disappeared. It's Clara. She is smiling at him. How is it that he had not recognized her? The current takes them to the far shore, which at this point in the river is a coral barrier. Clara invites him to follow her. She sees an underground cave, its opening just at water level, and she plunges because she wants to go into that cave. They emerge inside.

An old man is waiting for them with large towels. Her eyes are clear and lovely. As soon as they have dried themselves off, he explains the rules of the game to them. Clara answers the first set of questions without any difficulties whatsoever. But it is not so easy for Jonathan. Applause is heard rising in this rather unusual place. Clara is invited to step into another part of the cave, where there is something that looks exactly like a living room. It is comfortable, the atmosphere is hushed, easy going, one can hear the clinking of glasses, and the crackling of a television set.

Jonathan has to focus his energies on one last enigma. The answer seems silly to him. The question has to do with a TV series where the protagonists, living in today's world, are off on a quest for the Holy Grail. He is very anxious – stomach cramps coming on. The pain is unbearable, like the beating of his own heart. When suddenly he feels his body being taken in and fall like a ball of fire in the night. So Clara was indeed the woman in his dream! Slowly, Jonathan comes out of his daydream.

"A dream can often hide another dream," Leila says. "Like the warning signs at rail crossings in France: '*Un train peut en cacher un autre*,' right?" She adds: "A dream can't be as dark as it appears."

"Like the night-abyss, for instance," Jonathan says.

Leila smiles: "No doubt that expression means something. Night is not only a synonym for emptiness or absence. It can also refer to something that is coming forth, to the origin, if you like."

Jonathan's eyes light up: this pleases him immensely.

"Doesn't 'Leila' mean 'night' in Arabic?"

Leila acquiesces. She gets up, suddenly restless, troubled. She goes out onto the terrace. The landscape that lies before her is neither the Eiffel tower nor the Montparnasse tower with its lights, but the crest of some far-off hills burned by the sun. It is as if she can hear the deafening sound of the crickets, and see a broad burning plain that drinks up the shadows of night, with the sea vibrating against the sky far off at the horizon. A moment of eternity suspended, like an overhanging icon in her confused life. The iodized odour of the pine grove and this singular mixture of smoke and burning wood rises in successive waves – then suddenly Tom has put his index finger to her lips asking her to be quiet: her eyes glitter.

Leila does not hear right away the sounds coming from Jonathan's lips. The second time, the sounds are closer; she feels Jonathan's breath on her neck. Her smile is a bit strained, and she tries to avoid his gaze. Under the guise of seduction, this dinner unfolds like a ritual where coming together and parting seem to mesh in equal parts.

LEILA SEYYAD

16

"I don't know anything about you."

"It's better like that."

"Leila ... your name, is it because you were born during the night?"

"It was my Jordanian grandmother's given name."

"Do you know why your father left?"

"The war."

"Is this why, as a doctor, he wanted to take care of people?"

"Since he was a brilliant student, he was able to pursue his studies. Then he left his country."

"To go to Montreal?"

"Yes, that's it. He met my mother at the hospital during his internship. They got married almost immediately. She was a nurse there. My brother was born soon after."

She is silent. She would have wanted to continue, but she found it impossible to describe to Jonathan how things really were. How was it possible for her to speak to him about her father whom she loved yet hated so much at the same time? What happened had been entirely his fault. She had said nothing because of her mother. The letter that she had received from him so many years after he had left was a call for help. She had gone to try and find him. She first went to Algeria, then to Libya. Then she was off to Syria, to Iran and after that to Karachi. There the trail came to an end: in the dust of an open market in Karachi. So many years had gone by. She had sworn to bring him back, to get him to forsake his wild ideas. She felt she could do this now. She had moved heaven and earth. She had looked in all the hospitals. The refugee camps. In vain. That's where she could have found him, because that's exactly where he should have been. He had never given up on what he called "his people." It is this mission that had led him to Montreal. It was also that which had made him leave again some fifteen years later.

She can still see in her mind his massive silhouette, his white teeth, and that craziness in his eyes when he would get angry. He had wanted to take her with him. She had refused. So as not to become like her brother. So as not to become like him either. She sometimes wondered if she had even managed to avoid that? She had to admit to herself that she no longer knew.

"You are not real," Jonathan murmurs, looking at her intensely, like a pilgrim imploring a secret divinity to free him from a spell. "Tell me that you are not real. Tell me that you do not exist."

Leila lifts her head suddenly, briefly baring her white neck:

"I am but an image born out of your dream, a dream that you don't know what do with," she says in a mock dramatic style.

There is the hint of a smile on Leila's lips, a sweet smile that makes her all the more attractive.

"Because you are an intruder," Jonathan says. "An intruder in the chain of familiar images that I use to bring myself some kind of comfort, in order to go to sleep. This is why I am asking these questions. I want to know where my place is in this merry-go-round of yours. After all, I too am disrupting your little game!"

It is true that she is beautiful. He feels he can understand the strange battle that Leila has been waging ever since puberty: to keep at bay the desire that men have for her – though if anything, desire was exactly what transpired out of every pore of her own body. Her quest for spiritual things and her need to be altruistic were the natural shields she used to discourage the lust that men had for her. This was one of the reasons she chose nursing as a profession. It was less a desire to fit into the family tradition – there were so many doctors in the family – than as a means of protecting herself. It allowed her to retreat into herself as though into some kind of inner exile. And now here she was, trying to understand all of this.

And so Jonathan and Leila groped their way toward each other, neither of them really sure what separated them from the dream-self that each had constructed out of a need for protection. At this very moment and without any apparent logic, an image comes to Jonathan's mind. Something he had seen the evening before: the church of Val-de-Grâce in Paris. It was 7 p.m.: the pastel hues of twilight transforming its baroque façade, making it appear more beautiful than it really is. At this hour of the day, the traffic is still heavy. Nearby, the minimalist fountain gurgles with its false marble basins. A man comes and goes with a cell phone in his hand. The evening shadows are covering the friezes, enshrouding the immense columns on either side of the entrance way to the Church, hiding the heavy baroque volutes, while the dome remains out of reach, triumphant in the grand trappings of its past. Nothing more beautiful than this church burning in the setting sun, nothing more desirable than Leila's small body made iridescent in the fading light of eventide.

"What do you want?" Leila murmurs.

"You, of course."

"Me? I don't exist!"

17

Leila laughs. From the cultural centre in street below comes the syncopated rhythm of a tam-tam. The sound rises, with the obsessive clacking of the castanets, vaults over the terrace, and evaporates off and away into the night sky. In the distance, the Paris skyline has cleared-up. The humidity is dissipating with its mixture of perfumes: lilac, hawthorn, roses. Yet nothing can stop the breaker wave of sadness from coming down. Nothing can take the place of the emotions that move, skilfully and perilous, in the darkness of night.

18

Water is pouring over her skin.

The water flowing from the showerhead envelops Leila in a phosphorescent halo. Leila cries softly. She does not know whether she is crying from joy or from pain. The foul odour of silt and plaster mud rises from the marshes – it makes her want to throw up. She seems to be unable to fight off the stagnant waters that are seeping into her body.

She was wandering, stunned, in a moonlit clearing. She didn't want to go home. The cries of her father had frightened her; she could see his aged face, brilliant in the dark.

It is as if the water in the shower were streaming over her memories, memories that she wants cleansed forever of all those noxious images. These images have taken possession of her, like an assailant violating her body. They make it impossible for her to breathe. And yet in way she has consented to this, she has opposed nothing to this flood of recollections that is undermining her very existence. Oh, there was maybe that lightness of being that she would put on like a mask. She could always pretend that this was really her. But deep down she felt something like a madness stalking her. It was like an animal ready to jump on her – which is exactly what had happened to her brother.

"Leila?" Jonathan says quietly, worried. Her tears have moved him; her fragility makes him all the more vulnerable. And that is something that he can't stand. "Leila!" he says again, his voice pitched high because of the anxiety that's taken hold of him.

Jonathan can feel her lithe silhouette sliding under the sheets: he feels her cool body tremble and breathes in the lavender odour of her wet hair. Leila snuggles up to him. Peaceful. It was just an episode, a child's nightmare, vanishing as fast as it came.

Their meeting is part of a destiny now going through a set of variations. And in this particular variation there are a number of difficulties – like having to interpret a musical score upside down, something that would require that they remain calm, despite the fevered intensity gripping them. Words are of no use. The only thing that counts is their two bodies pressing against one another.

By the window, a deafening squawking greets the setting sun. The birds salute the declining light in a flurry of trills, cooings and chirpings. For a moment, the apartment is the epicentre of a sound storm. Then, silence. Leila's hair slides over Jonathan's body, brushes against his sex; Leila's mouth on his glans. His penis fills with blood, becomes root, becomes Trajan's column, which Leila licks with her tongue. Her teeth against his shaft. Jonathan falls back into a darkness filled with soft far-off lightning.

His skin is like a magnetic field. As his pleasure mounts, he forgets much of his past life as though absolved of it. He is transported out of this room filled with echoes, perfumed with their breaths, until the pleasure reaches its peak before receding as quickly as it came.

Leila has turned over in the bed; Jonathan can only see her hair and her white hips. It is as if she were dreaming. He falls asleep. After a moment, Leila can hear his low regular breathing: Jonathan is asleep. She is at peace.

19

SHE HAD ALWAYS THOUGHT that men would be able to define the space about her. Help her find her way in the world and give her some form of stability. She looks at Jonathan who is still asleep. He reminds her of her first lover. Their affair had lasted two years. A little longer than the others. But what if she were making the same mistake again? What if Jonathan was destined to be just another image to be put away along with all the others in that secret closet of hers that is jammed full of memories? But how was she to know for sure? She has already waited too long. There is only one way to solve this: offer herself up to him again completely. And in that way she would triumph over him, forcing him to send back to her the image of her real self. Jonathan wakes up, stretches. From the small chest of drawers he takes a rolled cigarette, lights it up, draws on it, then hands it to her. She inhales and the acrid taste of marijuana invades her mouth.

"How did she die?" she asks suddenly.

The question hits hard. Leila's head is resting on her hand. Her body is stretched out on the unmade bed. She looks like a nude out of a painting by Gauguin. Her eyes gaze at him, two sparkles of onyx, in the night. Jonathan is curled up. He no longer knows if he should be feeling guilty or just indifferent. It all seems so long ago now. Yet the hairline fracture is still very much there.

"I am sorry. I should not have!"

"No, on the contrary."

He lowers his eyes. And he begins to speak.

CLARA

20

I REMEMBER EVERYTHING: THE grey light falling from the window in the bedroom, the mess in the apartment, the music playing on the radio. It was something by Laurie Anderson. At the time, the world was being turned upside down, toppling over. The Berlin Wall had just fallen, and we felt we were being given a glimpse of a new era, a "new world order," as it was called then. There was a kind of excitement in the air that was palpable even for those who had never lived in Berlin or even seen it. The whole planet was jubilant over the fall of the Berlin Wall. The great tides of liberty were taking over. I had just arrived from work and wanted to ask my father – how terribly naïve of me! – a loan without interest; it was silly of me even to try since we spent most of our time fighting. And once again, he proved himself to be in utter bad faith about it all. I mean, the previous evening, he had accepted the idea, well, at least in principle, when he told me that buying this apartment was a great idea. But, the next day, he had changed his mind without offering any explanation. That's the way he was: to give hope, only to let you down the next day. He said that such turnarounds were actually good for me, that they would strengthen my character and teach me to count only on myself. In reality, all it did was to make me want to leave. And I think that that is what he wanted, too. I think what he feared the most was that I would take control over my own life. Whatever it was, I felt tired morally, psychologically, by this game he played where he tried in every possible way to manipulate me. All of this left me completely beside myself. That day, when I got home, I was in tears. I took my course notes and went out immediately. I was running late.

It had gotten much colder outside. It was autumn and already the city had fallen prey to a maelstrom of snow and fog drowning the mountain and the tall buildings. But I could care less; I was trying to allay the fury raging inside me. This always happened when I went to see the old man. Fortunately, there was Clara.

The bus arrived later than scheduled. At this hour of the day, there were just a few passengers. I sat near the back. A few stops later, a young man, hardly more than an adolescent, boarded the bus and sat in front of me. He was wearing battle fatigues, military gear thrown over his shoulder. His brush-cut made him look like a new recruit heading back to the barracks. Except that he was not really a soldier. Two small details gave him away: he was wearing tennis shoes and a pair of jeans instead of the regulation kaki pants. What struck me was how fidgety he was: he rummaged about in his bag, kept looking around him like a wolf caught in a trap ... I observed him, intrigued: his black shining eyes seemed to call for help. In a way, he looked very much like me, if it wasn't for my apparent calm. But he was the least of my worries: I really had to take a piss, and that's the only thing I could think about. In my haste, I hadn't even had a chance to go to the bathroom before leaving home. Fortunately, the university stop was not too far away.

We got off the bus together. The stranger asked me the way to the Polytechnic School of Montreal. His voice was so soft it was hard to hear. I asked him to repeat. This time his words were loud and clear: the fake soldier was furious that he had not been understand correctly the first time round. Despite his boorishness, I offered to take him there since it was on my way. He remained quiet the whole distance. A powerful animal energy emanated from him. An impression that was brought home to me because of his way of walking, striding like an automaton: he was behaving like a wolf at bay. I asked him if he was looking for someone in particular. "My sister," he said pointedly, as though nothing could be more obvious. I confess that I did not give it much thought. My mind was elsewhere. I had only a few minutes to find Clara whom I had not seen for a good two days. I left the man at the door of the university and ran to the cafeteria. Clara was waiting for me, seated at a table littered with a bunch of empty Styrofoam drinking cups. She had important things to tell me. When she got up to give me a kiss, the hubbub of the cafeteria with its odour of French fries evaporated as though by magic. Lovers are alone in the world, we say. An old cliché, for sure, but which was quite true for me at that instant. I was deeply in love.

She held me in her arms the whole time. Never had I seen her so radiant. When we finally sat down, she told me that her parents were ready to help pay for half the apartment on Maplewood Drive. Better still, that she had managed to convince the owner to lower the price he was asking for it. Clara was beaming and as for myself, well, I was plain dumbstruck. We had been looking for months for some way to finance all of this in order to buy the apartment. With this new price, it was now feasible. As long as we worked twice as hard. Since my father had been so obstinate, refusing to sign for me, I had asked an uncle who seemed ready to help. I was sure that he would back us, but he was often away, travelling all around the world. But none of this seemed so terribly urgent any more. Everything was falling into place so that we could live together. The next steps were of course: marriage, starting a family ... and not necessarily in that order. "And how about starting right away ...," Clara said, visibly happy that I should be bringing up such future prospects. When I saw her smile, I realized I had passed the test. That was of course "the other piece of good news." I was now completely hers – which pleased her no end! I kissed her. Destiny was pushing me in the right direction, so it seemed.

Classes were about to start, so we left holding each other's hand like school kids. I was on cloud nine. On the travelator, Clara pressed up against me and said something that had somewhat shocked me at the time. She said that if something were ever to happen to her, her large bookcase made of white pine and everything it contained would be mine. I found this to be out of place, especially after what she had just said to me. We were finally in front of room D-343. Among the students waiting there, there was that individual I had seen on the bus.

He was even more high-strung than when I'd left him. He still had all that gear with him. When I went by him, he didn't seem to recognize me. He was looking away toward the elevator and madly pacing back and forth as though to settle his nerves. The students were entering the classroom. I left Clara to go to the washroom finally. I had barely gone in when the young militiaman went behind me in a rush. Our eyes met for just a short moment. His face was cold, impassive. I took a long piss and didn't hear him leave.

I was about to exit the washroom when I noticed the gear on the floor in one of the stalls. The door to the stall had been left open. There was no one. I looked at the bag he'd left behind. My heart began beating wildly. I felt as though I was about to find proof of what I had somehow suspected ever since I had bumped into him earlier. Inside, there was a jumble of firearms of every imaginable calibre: magnums, colts, pump guns, even a few grenades. Fear gripped me. I began to run in the direction of room D-343. I had to get into that class before he did, whatever the cost. My hand was on the doorknob. I hesitated for a moment, then, I opened it quickly and felt something grab hold of my arm and pull me inside.

The door slammed shut behind me. The soldier was in the centre of the room. He was hooded, with an Uzi in his hand. Students were weeping and crying all around. He was yelling, shouting threats that made no sense whatsoever. When I saw the young men back away to the rear of the class and the young women line up in front of the blackboard, I could see what he was after. He was using his machine gun like a billhook to separate out the young men from the young women, roughly shoving those who were not cooperating. Clara went over and stood quietly with the women. The soldier was raving more than ever, talking of Gog and of Magog, of the Bible and of Armageddon. He yelled out that his mission was to accomplish the "great separation."

Suddenly, the maniac pronounced the name of a woman. He was blaming her for not being there. That it was all her fault. The confusion was total. The students were shaking, sobbing terribly. It was as if the people in that room had entered a universe where the gravitational forces had multiplied tenfold. The slightest movement became impossible – it was as if we had to fight off the weight of ten atmospheres. Just breathing was painful. The two groups were now clearly separated. No one could move. We were all paralyzed with fear.

How long did this last? No more than a few moments, I'm sure. But for me it seemed to be an eternity. In that horrible scene there was a "before" and an "after," a line separating life from death. But how is one to find where that line lay exactly? Time had changed its nature. It had taken on the mask of this hooded individual. And he was forcing us to look dead on at our destiny.

My attention was of course totally focussed on Clara. She had already understood what was about to happen. I will never forget what I saw in her eyes. It was decomposing in a thousand sequences that contained our potential life together: our joys, our pains, our disputes, the children that we would have had, our disappointments, the passing of time, our old age … Then, suddenly, I made an unexpected move. I stepped forward and I screamed: "No!" loud enough for him to hear.

THE COINCIDENCE

This caught the crazed man by surprise. In the space of an instant he turned and all the tension in room seemed to settle on me in a terribly concentrated way. Just a few metres separated me from him. I had opened my hand to ask him to give me his weapon. It was within reach. I could see his eyes through his hood: two small burning black pebbles that moved very quickly: I saw an immense solitude, the frightened gaze of a little boy terrorised by a will that was not his own.

But that's not the only thing I saw. I saw much more: an April day long ago in Alger la blanche, the early evening panorama of the port of Candie, the ruins of Tipasa, the threads of destiny that come together only to dissolve here in this precise instant, under this hooded gunman's stare. And so did history come to fruition like something dreadful dredged up from the floors of an unexplored ocean. And then I saw Clara on a beautiful spring day in the apartment on Maplewood Dive. I saw hatred, then love, then hatred again. I saw the magnetic field which protected me, I saw the equatorial jungle as I had once seen it from the Sun Pyramid in the Yucatan peninsula – then I saw the altar that had been used for the Aztec sacrifices: this is what room D-343 had become.

And I saw the sacrifice that was about to begin, the time that remained, I saw the inconceivable, the LAW, its violence, I felt that at that moment I WAS THE LAW, its instrument, its inscrutable Power, and I grew afraid and I backed away. Time had shrugged off its weight and was now accelerating wildly. Time no longer had any need of me. I was ejected from its circle. I had become the Moment of moments, but I had not seized it. Time would now accomplish its task without me; things could resume their course just as the intruder had decided. The crazed man looked away, his eyes no longer interested in me.

Then everything went really fast. The first volley of shots hit the first eight students; with the second volley, five other students went down. Clara was one of them. Blood was spurting everywhere over the walls. A brutal silence fell. It was like a veil that is torn and it is in this rending that the demented individual – his name was Thomas as I was to find out later – suddenly realized what he had just done. He took off his hood, called one last time, almost affectionately, the name of that girl, put the barrel of the 575 magnum in his mouth and fired. Maybe he looked at me when he pulled the trigger, I don't know, the fact remains that ever since that day his eyes have never ceased to haunt me.

After? After … what is there to say … reality went on automatic pilot. I entered into a state of hypnosis, a state that is still mine today. The truth is that I have never accepted Clara's death. For me, it was a nightmare from which I would awaken: Even after the shots on that day, Clara was alive on the ground, as though sleeping by my side. I bent over her where she lay and murmured to her that I would never leave her – ever.

Two powerful arms then tore her from me. The cries, the weeping, the hysterical laughter, the lamentations formed a tapestry of strident soundless sounds, sharp and low and somehow muffled. I was going forward like a zombie. I was unable to speak. I could not understand all this agitation around me. All of this was just so much fiction, the repetition of a well-rehearsed made-up scene so that TV viewers could enjoy a cold sweat thanks to the evening news. Reality could not be this. Not this. Not like this. The proof: soon Clara would get up from the stretcher in the ambulance to come with me to pick up the keys to our new apartment. Later, I would tell her about this bad dream I had had, and she would laugh her crystalline laugh that moved me so; and life would start all over again as though nothing had happened.

21

Jonathan talks without so much as a pause, as though in some altered state. He emerges from a night filled with shadows. He has the impression that he is coming out of a long period of drowsiness. For the first time, he glimpses a faint light that will allow him to take a few steps forward – finally. It was already so long ago when, on December 9, 1989, he entered that long dark tunnel. Never had he confided himself to anyone and especially not in this kind of trance. He did not even notice that Leila had lain down, and that she was shaking her head vigorously as though trying to deny something.

He moves closer to her, murmuring a banality of the kind: "All that is in the past now." But Leila fights back.

"Don't touch me! Don't ever touch me again!" she screams.

Leila is suddenly transformed into a wounded animal, an animal that senses it has been led into some kind of a trap. She gets up, grabs her clothing and leaves the room, slamming the door shut behind her. Jonathan can hear her moaning and muttering out of anger, cursing against whatever fate it was that brought her to this apartment. Coming to, Jonathan puts on his bathrobe. Leila is getting ready to leave. He blocks the way, grabs her wrist, takes the key out of her hand and slips it into his own pocket. He wants to understand, he asks for some explanation. Her answer is to jump on him, scratching away at him like a wild cat trying to get the key back. They fight, roll on the ground. Finally, Jonathan nails her to the floor. Her black eyes are brilliant in the night. She is all in a sweat, breathless. Finally overcome, she goes limp.

"You don't understand," Leila laments, exasperated. "You can't."

Jonathan looks at her as though he is seeing her for the very first time. All he really knows of this woman is the sinuous shape of her body, of her hips, the softness of her stomach and that familiar voice which had confused him for a moment on the telephone. But now something else or rather *someone* else was coming to life before his eyes – like some hard demented truth suddenly appearing, rising out of a cache of illusions. Jonathan had lived a life where semblance ruled, but now the moment had come. And somehow Leila knows this, too. She frees herself from Jonathan's arms and seeks refuge in a dark corner of the terrace behind the acanthus and eucalyptus.

She is no longer a panther; she is a frightened doe, a wounded fawn that can leap at the bat of an eye. He can't see her in the half-light, he can only hear her voice, a reedy voice that pours over and around the objects on the terrace. It is a voice that emits a chant of incomprehensible words, a kind of child's language, a mixture of French and Arabic. There is something in her words about the desert, about her older brother whom she had not yet named, but whose name now comes back in a loop like a mantra. She repeats that he is the assassin, that it is her fault ... *her* fault. At first Jonathan refuses to understand. This just can't be. This coincidence, it's just too much. He moves closer to the plants like one approaches the cave of a Soothsayer: filled with a sacred terror and respect. He hears her panting and these words repeated like a cantilena: "Tom kills the young women ... All the young women ... Tom has killed the young women ... all the young women ... it was for her. Because of her. He was crazy. It was her fault. It was all her fault."

Her moaning makes up a far away language that rises in the night like a prayer, a confession searching for an improbable absolution. Once the initial shock is over, Jonathan becomes receptive, accepting this bizarre revelation like a sign of destiny. His distress has turned into some kind of inner jubilation. That which had bound itself on that December day in 1989 might finally be loosened on this eve of Pentecost. Jonathan comes to. "Leila! Come. Come out of from behind there," he says. He can barely make out her body all curled up against the wall, like the little girl that she has become again. But slowly Leila's voice begins, rises out of the rings of delirium, trying to make contact, trying to lay hold onto something, anything for support.

THOMAS

22

"On that day, I had a class, but I didn't go ... I was afraid ... I was terrorized ... He had changed so much ... I could no longer recognize him ... Maybe if I had been there ..."

"What happened?" Jonathan asks.

There is a silence. Leila tries to put some sort of order in the memories she has of that day, find the right words, the right tone ...

"So many things were said ... the press ... His personal diaries were published ... He was not a violent person ... His fascination for weapons came later ...

"Later?"

"After the death of his father. Our father had been a taciturn man, quick-tempered, irascible ... But ... the truth ... Even if he was my brother, even if we never really know the people who are close to us ... even after all these years, I don't think that he had anything against women."

"So why did he do it?"

"I don't know. Maybe he wanted to free himself form the influence of his father … When he was a young boy, his father would beat him, especially when he was drunk or when he came home from work with the worries of his job weighing on his mind. Though Tom hated his father, this hatred never led to an open conflict between them. It lay buried deep inside him. The violence that our father dealt us was so insidious: it reduced us to stone, leaving us unable to reply, unable to strike back. We simply could not react or counter it in any way. It is true that my brother was very young then. And when our father left, we were left with all that stored up anger and frustration locked up inside us. Had he stayed, maybe Tom would have been able to stand up to him, and in this way find a way out. But this violence was old. It came from way beyond, through generations of men before my father.

"My father exercised a true ascendency over us. He had obtained his diploma as a medical doctor through sheer force of will and against the very will of the Seyyad family. He even left his own family over that. In other circumstances and at another time, he would have been like so many other immigrants who more or less easily melted into the Western model.

"But my father had never accepted the ways of West. He was too proud – proud of his privileges that were like an entitlement, proud too of his bloodline. He could not understand what he called 'Western World laxity' and could not stand that his children could fall for that. But he knew that he could not oppose himself to it. And so, my brother and I were submitted to a strict discipline. Moreover, he was terribly jealous. My mother and I were not allowed to leave the house, we were basically locked up. He would beat her regularly. My mother felt she no longer knew the man she had married fifteen years before.

"When she decided to ask for a divorce, my father had already left the house. His leaving us really upset my brother, he was truly distressed, angry. He broke everything that had belonged to our father, everything he could lay his hands on in the house. My mother was obliged to take refuge in her neighbour's home. He was sent to a psychiatric hospital and tried to commit suicide twice. When he came back to the house, he was no longer the same. He took up his studies again, but his heart was just not in it. He was only sixteen years old. It was at that time that his fascination for weapons began. He said that he wanted to make a career in the army. He tried to enrol, but he was declared unfit for service because of his psychiatric history. He was very frustrated. He answered to whoever would listen that he would do his own training, that he would create his own militia to find his father and shoot him down."

"Where had your father gone?"

"We don't know. We think he went back to his native village. After the country had been closed to tourists because of all the assassination attempts, he was sighted elsewhere, in Beyrouth, then in Karachi ... A few months after he had left, Tom decided to change his family name from Seyyad to that of his mother: Lacroix. He thought that in this manner he could wipe his father out of his memory, but this did not stop him from becoming like him: a madman."

"How do you know?"

"I often asked myself questions about what we had inherited from our father's side. On the one hand, he left us his stubbornness, and on the other hand this muted violence that had managed to live on from one generation to the next. My father was a man trapped by his own past. He was able to free himself at least for a while by leaving his country, emigrating to acquire the education that would allow him to rise from the ranks. My mother often said that my brother had inherited his violence, and I his stubbornness. I would beg her not to say this kind of nonsense – it only served to alienate us further from Tom. It could only intensify his anger all the more.

"To him, that is for Tom, knowledge was a delusion. Tom believed that the freedom that his father believed he had acquired through his studies was not real; it was fake. Just like my father had done, Tom forbade me to study. It displeased him immensely that I should want to "follow in our father's footsteps," as he put it. As for me, I simply wanted out. I no longer wanted anything to do with this fate that seemed to be hovering over our family."

"And your mother?"

"Now, she was something else. She too was a product of madness – her own family's madness. It is only now, with the passing of time, that I have come to realize this. She had internalized the suffering of her family who were mainly peasants. In the way she would stiffen when my father beat her, in the way she put up her arms to protect herself, in the way her eyes became filled with terror, I could see the generations of women who worked hard, nearly killing themselves, to raise big families in utter destitution. My father and my mother were both deeply wounded beings. Maybe that's why they were attracted to each other. We, their children, are the fruit of a double failure."

She pauses.

"Every day I think of my brother. His adolescent face, his empty gaze, his halting gait. Every day I tell myself that I could have done something to prevent this massacre; I should have, it was my duty. It's what he would have wanted: that I stop him. But I was afraid like you were when you stood up to my brother in that classroom. I turned a blind eye and a deaf ear to all of it. I lacked courage."

Leila stops. She remains prostrate, mumbling against the wind that is making the bells tinkle in the eucalyptus.

"God of the winds," she says in a low voice, "absolve my sin, take it with you far away, very far from this world of ours that has lost all countenance, all reference points, that has forgotten the law, your law."

She continues.

"When Tom said that he was going to kill in order to root out the evil in his life, I did not really believe him. We had so often heard him speak grandly about his 'apocalypse' that my mother and I had become impervious to it all – indifferent, anaesthetised. To be truthful, our greatest fear was that he might take it out on himself. I had tried to convince him to go back to the psychiatric ward, but he would not hear of it. I tried to warn the medical staff looking after him, but my request – I found this out later through the press – had only been registered the day after the tragedy. He had changed so much in so little time.

"I think he was jealous of me. I was getting on with my life, studying engineering. His distress turned to hatred against me. And I just did not know how to help him anymore. I was so alone. As for my mother ... she ... my mother could no longer take it. Depression, absence. That was her answer to the violence that was boiling up from deep inside her son. He had become a stranger to her – just as she had become a stranger to herself. She didn't really know who she was or what she was. And it is this kind of inertia that in a curious way kept her tied, kept her connected to her son – because he expressed the same aversion toward the world that she herself felt. All through this, my brother would say that he was tired of seeing her body and her face growing old, that he himself was good for nothing, incapable of loving, that he did not want to die before having wreaked revenge, and so on and on.

"The day before the event, before the tragedy, we had had a violent disagreement over the fact that I had a boyfriend, a university student like myself. He wanted to kill him. I told my brother that he was raving mad, that I would call the police, that he had no right to ruin my life like this – that it was quite enough that he was ruining his own life. He wanted to hit me, but he held himself back. After which, in a very ostentatious almost ritualistic manner, he decreed that I was no longer his sister. In his eyes, I had become a slut like all the others, a whore whom he would punish.

"I shrugged my shoulders, and left, slamming the door behind me. And I went directly to my boyfriend's apartment. He was not expecting me. We made love. I stayed overnight. He had not hoped for so much! The following day, I had a class, but I was riddled with fear. I kept my boyfriend in bed. We made love again. I no longer wanted to know who I was. My behaviour surprised my boyfriend. Robert was his name. The previous night I played the game of holier than thou ... This amused him at first. Then I saw that it was beginning to worry him. Me, I was insulting him, provoking his male pride, telling him that he didn't have any balls. He twisted my arm at first, wanting me to submit. In a kind of a game, I put the belt around his neck. I must have tightened it too much because he hit me hard and I landed on the floor.

"Robert said that I had become crazy, that I wanted to kill him. It's possible, mind you. I think that, in my imagination, it was my brother whom I was strangling. It was about then that we heard the sirens because Robert's apartment was just in front of the University. At first there were only a few sirens; then there were others and in no time at all it had become totally deafening. We had the impression that the whole sector was going up in flames. We opened the window: dozens of police cruisers, ambulances had arrived from all over the place. Stroboscopic lights illuminated the darkened sky – it was the end of the afternoon and it was December.

"Policemen and ambulance personnel were running toward the big cement building: there seemed to be dozens of them; others were cordoning off the sector; police barriers were being set up hurriedly. Robert put on a bathrobe and went out to ask what was going on. Neighbours told him that a killing had taken place just in front. We put on the TV. Regular programming had been interrupted. A news flash described the tragedy that had just occurred. Suddenly, amidst the confusion of ambulances, amidst all the cries and the "testimonies," I saw my brother's photo. I was paralyzed. I broke down, and I cried out of rage, out of a sense of utter helplessness.

"At first Robert could not understand, but when he made the connection between me and the person in that photo, instead of trying to comfort me, he chased me away kicking me and not wanting to see me ever again. He threw my clothes on the landing. You could see the terror in his eyes. I got dressed in the hallway as best I could, shedding all the tears from my body. The neighbours were staring at me; they were completely taken aback; they thought we had had a fight. I could care less. I had other things on my mind – obviously. I knew instantly that Tom had done what he did because he had not found me in that class: I was after all supposed to be there.

"I went out into the night filled with the wailing of sirens. I did not know where to go. I could not breathe. I did not want to go back home. Some policemen saw me wandering about in tears and thought that I knew someone who had died in the tragic events. They asked if I needed help. I left right away.

"The whole sector had been cordoned off. I went into a coffee house; I asked for a double brandy and swallowed it bottoms up. After that, I called Maria, my best friend, and asked her if I could spend the night with her. It is only some time over the next days that I decided to call my mother. She was beside herself and feared that I was among the victims. I was questioned right away by the authorities. I had to tell them my whereabouts on the previous evening; Robert was called in and he corroborated the fact that I had been with him. He did however take the time to lay a charge of attempted murder against me. But he quickly withdrew it.

"I was put in temporary detention and was obliged to undergo a psychological assessment of sorts before I was let go for Tom's funeral. When his body was given back to us, my mother and I buried him hurriedly, secretively, like we were all pariahs. My mother and I never saw each other again. Rather than bringing us together, the pain was to separate us forever. I hated her for having overprotected him, to have kept him under her skirts, when he should have been allowed to fly with his own wings.

"Fly with my own wings, that is precisely what I did. I did a complete turn-about in my studies. I left engineering and went into nursing. I even went to a university in a totally different part of the country where no one knew me. Then I left for the Sudan and later for Rwanda. It is there, in Rwanda, that I met my future husband who was a volunteer in a non-governmental organization like me. We got married right away. But this marriage was more of a convenience allowing me to cut myself off from my past. To be truthful, I did not love Peter. He seemed however to take this situation in his stride. My husband was a decent man if a bit boring. But he would not hurt a fly. That worked fine for me. The idea of doing some work in the theatre came to me at that time."

Leila was quiet again. In the interval, her voice had become steady. Her fears seemed to have abated. Leila could thus finally come out of her "den," cat-like and shining. The down on her skin was still vibrating with traces of memory. Her eyes seemed large, with streaks of mascara running down, Arlequina-like.

"No way that I am going to let you go," Jonathan murmurs between his teeth. "You have not told me everything, little panther.

"At the beginning, my brother and I were like allies, setting up a barrier against my father's anger and my mother's madness. It was our way of challenging the violence in our family or at least it was our attempt to keep it at bay. He was five years older than I."

"Seriously?" Jonathan asks, as though this difference in age is the most important thing of all.

But she doesn't answer and just keeps going, dead set on revealing the past.

"A complicity took place between us, one beyond the simple erotic games between brothers and sisters. It took unexpected turns. We lived on an island. We were alone. My father had decided to keep us away from the city which he considered 'dangerous.' He had set up a startling garden. My brother and I were the sovereigns of this curious natural reserve situated about an hour from the centre of the city. We stayed there for a good five years, right up to my 17th birthday. At the very centre of this island there was an abandoned factory. The dilapidated warehouses near the factory seemed so immense to us.

"Thomas was like a fish in water there. He invented a thousand games. He had a vivid imagination. But his forays, or should I call it his "theatre," sometimes led him to do some really sick things. One day, in the factory, we found a container filled with acid. Thomas plunged our cat alive in the acid. He wanted to obtain a complete skeleton. He had got it in his head to collect the bones of small animals for the class he was taking in zoology. Already, when he was younger, Thomas was not like the others. He would get up late or really early and then disappear. Sometimes for days at a time. Then he would reappear as though nothing had happened.

"He was very secretive. Even to me, he said nothing. Whenever his father would ask him what he was up to, it always ended up with a thrashing: his father would beat him with his belt buckle, then would lock him up in the basement. He could go for several days at a time without saying a word, barely eating. When I would go and see him with a plate of food, he would push it away. His gaze worried me, the way he just stared. A strange light burned in his eyes, as though he was seeing right through us and beyond. He said that I would be his aide-de-camp, that he would always stay with me, that we would never leave each other.

"One day, he brought me to the other end of the island. We went into a small room in the basement adjacent to the factory, a room that he had furnished with a broken down sofa and some old chairs. It was a miniature home. This is how I found out where he would hide when we would call him at the end of the day. The night was warm, it was the month of May. My parents had spent the day fighting and had gone to bed early. As a result, they had forgotten that it was my birthday. I had just turned fifteen. But Thomas remembered. He had prepared a cake in his hide-away. He who was so clumsy, so unpredictable, showed that he could actually be very thoughtful: he had gotten hold of some wine, which he served in tall champagne glasses, a wedding gift that our parents had received. We drank. Then he gave me a guided tour of his 'laboratory'. One could have said that he was about to lift off so diaphanous and light did he seem. He told me to drink. He told me strange things."

She shakes her head.

"It was all at once beautiful and mysterious and terrifying."

She shrugs her shoulders.

"It was like a curse. It went something like this." She raises her voice. It quivers a little, then hardens: "'We must pursue ... the way beyond the fleece of the pine and cedar trees ... the maples, the wild cherry trees, the ash trees, beyond the lakes and the rivers filled with trout.'"

Leila stops for a moment.

"I can't remember it word for word, of course. I can only recall bits and pieces. Something like this: 'The great polar island is calling us ... the nocturnal sun radiates on the chalice filled with the black blood of the continent. Thus will come the glacier-like purity. For he shall come back ... Then all will be as before. And the spirit of ice ... the spirit of hardened water will fill each crevasse exulting in its royal solitude ... its progression toward the slow and sovereign sea. Purifying. For nothing will be left of man. The land will exult, finally liberated of its stain, of its blasphemous pride ... and it will find again its original state. The new man will wash himself in the lustral waters and he will be able to accomplish his destiny in the virginity of the snows that burn and purify. The diamond shape is the archangel of the annunciation. Its name is Mary. It is from her that I received the message to purify the world; re-establish the lost object, the broken circle.'

"At the time, I was troubled. The feeling that he took himself for a shaman became clear, but only much later. It is true that I had drunk more than I should have. We were looking at the boats go by on the river. Then he took me in his arms, he was sweating profusely. His voice had changed. He told me that the time had come. He undressed me and we made love for the first time that night. We made love again. My parents were never aware of this of course, they never knew. He remained my lover until my eighteenth year, long after our parents had separated."

Leila stops talking. She raises her eyes and adds:

"I have the feeling that he never accepted that we separated from each other; that I saw other boys: he was exclusive, possessive. On that 9th of December he had summoned me."

A shiver runs down Jonathan's spine. The meaning of the dream he had had this morning now seems obvious. The time has come. Dread mixes with joy, with the excitement of finally being able to accomplish one's destiny, to be able to take hold of it. A breach opens up in his life and he sees a light: it is the light of the apartment on Maplewood Drive, and in this morning light of May, Clara's face emerges more radiant than ever, almost physical.

Jonathan accepts what the luminous machine of destiny has brought him. He is but one of its many working wheels, but he feels that it is now showing him the way. It's useless to resist, he has only to let himself be led to his room. He closes the door behind him: he has to get ready. Leila hardly noticed that he'd left the room. She nonetheless asks him what he is doing. He answers from the bedroom that he is getting dressed. Nothing could be more normal since he was naked in his bathrobe! It is almost dawn. It'll be the day of the Pentecost, the feast of the Spirit, of the wind of the Paraclete, of the holy congregation.

Leila plays the fawn; she has become this animal fetish, with its white powder puff of a tail; she moves quickly from ashtray to ashtray, depositing the ashes from her cigarettes. Since the story has entered its final phase, she has begun to smoke again. She smoked Jonathan's pack of cigarettes, the whole of it. The curls of smoke are like a tapestry. When he returns from the bedroom, Jonathan pushes back this filmy curtain in a casual off-handed though solemn manner. He looks superb dressed like this, all in black, with his black silk shirt and his mandarin collar. He has never been so handsome! Even Leila can't get over it. He is a different man, surely!

Jonathan goes out onto the balcony and leans against the handrail to look at Paris. There are no clouds in the sky. The day is dawning. A little more and the great rout will get under way again. The city will come alive. The urbane buzz will begin to thrive.

Jonathan thinks of the multitude of life stories behind each of those luminous dots that cover the city. It is like a swarm of reddish-blue fireflies hovering low over Paris. Jonathan feels Leila's presence by his side.

"Strange that we have met."

"We could have fallen in love, had lived together, had children …"

"It almost happened."

"Almost."

"And now?"

"We have reached the conclusion."

"What do you mean?"

"What has been tied must now be untied."

Jonathan hands her a revolver that he has taken out of his pocket. Leila understands immediately; she pushes the weapon away. She jumps to the other end of the room, then returns to face Jonathan.

"Why?"

"To accomplish the separation."

"Have you become crazy? Crazy like my brother?"

Jonathan smiles.

"But ... I am your brother!"

She starts back.

"No."

"Why refuse what you've known all along."

"Do it yourself if you want, but let me go."

"If I fire the shot, it would not have the same meaning. What's more, it is *you* who want to separate from me, not the other way around."

"That's just a lot of gibberish."

"In the art of hunting, there is the prey and there is the hunter: the one who is chased and the one who chases. You cannot resolve your life if you do not choose to be the one or the other."

"This is nonsense."

"According to your destiny, you are the hunter. Before you, your brother was the hunter. He remained the hunter even after his death. It is time that you get rid of him. You must chase him away. You have to kill him."

Jonathan again hands her the revolver.

"You are not my brother."

Jonathan smiles ironically.

"I can force you to hate me."

"And how would you do that?"

"Like this."

He slaps her so hard that she is sent reeling several metres back. She holds her hand to her cheek in an attempt to soothe the pain. The black, immense mass of Jonathan moves toward her. Leila's face is sweating. Her eyes are big. An insidious voice rises:

"What did your father do on that day when he caught the both of you?"

Leila begs him not to insist, not to continue this insufferable questioning, but he won't listen.

"He was black with rage, wasn't he?"

Leila doesn't respond.

"Answer me!"

"Yessssss!"

"What did he do then?"

"Stop!"

"I will tell you what he did. He sent Thomas off, and then he tried to lay his hands on you. You were running all over the place. Like today, right?"

"Right!"

His face is now just a few centimetres from hers.

"Noooooooo?!"

Leila can no longer see Jonathan through the tears streaming down her face. She feels a presence and this presence is only too familiar to her. The gestures decompose in a sort of modern ballet where the bodies surface against the light. The chase adds to the excitement. Jonathan has again become a hunter. And Leila his prey. A classic? Unless it's the other way round.

"How did he grab you? Like this ..."

He immobilizes her, she is face down; he himself has become a stranger. He screams. He does not recognize his own voice. The *other* has taken possession of him, trashing him around like a puppet. He has become this crazed man who feels the weight of the whole community pressing down on him. It is this community that is commanding his movements.

"This is what your old man did to you, isn't it? Thomas fled, did he not? He left you alone with him."

Jonathan unbuttons his fly. The desire to possess her rises in him again. He wants this woman furiously. He wants her to submit, to be humiliated. He holds her firmly to the ground and bites her neck until it bleeds. To be freer in his movements, he puts the gun on the floor right up close, but was this planned? Leila gives one last push and grabs the gun. She holds it with both hands aiming it at him, she unlocks it, Jonathan moves back.

"I hate you, you are crazy just like he was."

She rises to her feet, walks backward.

"The keys," she demands.

With an ironic smile, Jonathan makes them clink in his pocket and says that they will be hers "after". Even better. He takes advantage of the situation to give her the final instructions: the keys that should be left in the jar by the door, the envelope containing her money and that she must not forget to take with her; the fingerprints that she must be sure to remove; the revolver that she must put in his left hand …

Jonathan is quiet now. Has he said everything? He looks at her with an air of melancholic triumph. Silence. The early morning air is diaphanous, strangely vivifying.

"We are on the day of the Pentecost. We move toward the Spirit."

Then suddenly one hears the light familiar vibration, this kind of far-off, indefinite ringing.

"Listen. You hear it?"

He smiles.

"It is the little music of the spheres. It is the signal. Now is the moment."

EPILOGUE

No one heard the shot go off, nor the body collapse on the floor of the terrace. From the outside, everything seemed normal. The wind rose, the Tibetan bells rang with these pearl-like, spindly notes that Jonathan loved so much because they reminded him, God knows why, of the Maplewood apartment where he never got to live. What follows belongs to a short news item. The police got there on the following day; the taxi driver who was supposed to drive Jonathan to the airport had tipped them off. A security perimeter was set up. The forensics expert simply registered the date of death. The neighbours provided conflicting testimonies. Some said that they had seen a young woman leave running out of the apartment in the early hours of the morning. Others maintained that there had been no one else with him at that hour of the night. Without any proof, the authorities classified it. Suicide. This is how the life of Jonathan Vincent Hunt, eldest son of Nathanaël Hunt, ended at 4 rue du Pavillon de chasse on this day of the Pentecost.

The hunt has come to an end. *Requiescat in pace.*

About the Author

FULVIO CACCIA is the author of four novels, including *La Coïncidence* (Triptych 2005), *Golden Eighties*, a short story collection (Balzac, 1994), and six collections of poetry, among them: *Italie et autres voyages* and *Aknos* (Guernica Editions), winner of the 1994 Governor-General's Award for Poetry. He is also the author of three essays on literature and modern society. Caccia is the founding director of the Observatory of Cultural Diversity in France. His website: www.fulvio-caccia.org.

About the Translator

ROBERT RICHARD is the author of a novel – *A Johnny Novel* (The Mercury Press, 1997) – as well as books on Dante and Sade. His book, *L'Émotion européenne*, won the Eva-le-Grand prize for best nonfiction of 2005. Richard, who resides in Montreal, served as the music critic for the *Ottawa Citizen* between 1976 and 1981.

Printed in February 2015
by Gauvin Press,
Gatineau, Québec